Trail of Rogues

Trail of Rogues

Fred Grove

A DOUBLE D WESTERN

DOUBLEDAY

New York   London   Toronto   Sydney   Auckland

A DOUBLE D WESTERN
PUBLISHED BY DOUBLEDAY
a division of Bantam Doubleday Dell Publishing Group, Inc.
666 Fifth Avenue, New York, New York 10103

DOUBLE D WESTERN, DOUBLEDAY,
and the portrayal of the letters DD
are trademarks of Doubleday, a division of
Bantam Doubleday Dell Publishing Group, Inc.

Library of Congress Cataloging-in-Publication Data

Grove, Fred.
Trail of rogues/Fred Grove.—1st ed.
p.   cm.—(Double D western)
I. Title.
PS3557.R7T73   1993
813'.54—dc20   92-30525
CIP

ISBN 0-385-46822-9
Copyright © 1993 by Fred Grove
All Rights Reserved
Printed in the United States of America
April 1993
First Edition

10 9 8 7 6 5 4 3 2 1

Trail of Rogues

One

Mesilla, New Mexico Territory, July 1867.

To this little frontier town the obliging proprietor of the El Paso stage station had directed Jesse Alden Wilder—if, the man said, disapproving, a person was foolish enough to head out for Arizona, dangerous as conditions were on the trail, particularly the long stretch from Mesilla to Fort Cummings, where Apaches even attacked wagon trains, and God help the lone traveler. Furthermore, he said, Jesse's blood-bay saddler would be like a beacon to thieving Apache eyes.

Mesilla, just a few jumps from the Rio Grande, was once part of Mexico, sold after the Mexican War in the Gadsden Purchase. *A victim of Manifest Destiny,* Jesse thought, feeling sympathy for a country he both understood and sometimes deplored. *President Benito Juárez would never have agreed to the giveaway, made virtually at gunpoint, if he'd been in power instead of that squanderer Santa Anna.*

But riding into the busy plaza, he saw that it was still mainly a Mexican village, which pleased him. *You don't change a place's culture and people simply by signing a piece of paper.*

He tied the red horse and pack mule at the first saloon's hitching rack, aware that he drew curious stares from idling Anglo-Americans and Mexicans. Taking his sheathed Spencer carbine, he went inside, found an opening at the long bar and ordered tequila. A sip and he decided he'd had better, but it was passable.

To his surprise, a slurred voice on his right said, "A white man drinkin' tequila? What the hell!"

"Beats rotgut whiskey," Jesse said.

The drunk took affront. "Whiskey's a white man's drink—what I drink." He squared around.

Jesse was worn out, with war-torn Mexico not many days behind him. Wearily, he reined in a quick retort and said evenly, "Every man to his own taste, I reckon, or what he can get out here. In Mexico, the tequila's better than the cheap whiskey sent across the border. You might try it. I'll buy you a drink." Before the man could protest, Jesse signaled the bartender. Sliding the other's drink before him, Jesse held up his glass and said, "Here's to peaceful times and better whiskey."

The drunk downed his drink, blinked, as if surprised at the quality, wet his lips, nodded, and muttered, "Now, frien', I'll buy you a white man's drink."

To refuse would be to provoke a fight, which was the last thing Jesse needed. They drank in unison. Like the tequila, the whiskey possessed no noble origin, but it was passable. He was nodding to that when from outside he heard a shouted, "Ride 'im! Hang on!" An instant knowing sent him rushing outside.

A man astride the red horse was bouncing around while he clung desperately to the saddlehorn. Jesse stopped. Under different circumstances he might have been amused. Well, it wouldn't last long.

Head low, squealing and pitching left and right, landing stiff-legged every time, violently snapping the rider's head and shoulders, the horse suddenly switched ends. The man left the saddle like a missile, his hat sailing off like a giant leaf. He landed with a dusty plop. The idlers laughed. The would-be rider, a white man, lay there for several seconds, stunned, hacking for wind.

The horse, reins dragging, head lowered, watched him warily.

With the idlers still laughing, the man jerked to his feet. "I'll ride that copper-colored son of a bitch yet."

Jesse went to his horse and took the reins. "You couldn't if you tried. He was tied or you couldn't have mounted him. No stranger can ride this horse."

"I will."

"You won't get the chance."

"Try and stop me."

Jesse drew the carbine. "One more step, you're a dead horse thief, I promise you. That's what you were tryin' to do—steal my horse." Earing back the hammer with a distinct click, he brought the Spencer level.

The man tensed forward, then seemed to slow up on second thought.

Behind Jesse, in front of the saloon, a man said, "I believe I'd take this feller at his word, Gat. Come on. This horse can't be rode, nohow."

The voice belonged to an owlish little character showing a gap-toothed grin and bloodshot eyes, who spoke in a wheedling way as he moved past Jesse. "He wasn't gonna steal your horse, sir. He just wanted to ride 'im, he's so purty."

"I don't think so," Jesse said.

After retrieving his hat, the one called Gat dusted it against his thigh, glared at Jesse, muttered, "All right, Clinch," but still delayed as if to make something of it. He was a stocky individual, with a long flat nose and a broad, hard-featured face framed by a black beard. Still glaring, he sulked across the plaza with the little man.

In town only fifteen minutes and already two run-ins with white men. Jesse shook his head wryly. As he turned to his horse, his anxious eyes sought the red ribbon. It was still in the black mane, undamaged, and there it would stay until it wasted away. Sight of it brought back a memory that would never be far from his mind. He let it linger for a run of moments before shutting it out.

He was hungry, but a man looked after his stock before seeing to his own needs. He bought oats and bran at a store near the stage station a block away and fed from nose bags. That done, he found a little hole-in-the-wall Mexican restaurant crowded with travelers, and filled up on brown beans, chili con carne, tortillas, and strong black coffee.

Afterward, whiling away time in the shade of the stage station, idly watching the clutter of a small encampment of ox-drawn wagons camped across the road, he sensed the pulse of the village as an observer and by the hum of conversation around him. Mesilla was the jumping-off point not only for the immigrant trail to California, but also for the gold camps at Pinos Altos, in the mountains northwest of Fort Cummings. Every man around him seemed to be waiting for something: two eager prospectors talking of gold and silver strikes, a gambler dressed in black broadcloth, probably bound for the mining camps, some apparent drifters, a man who chatted about business prospects, thus a merchant, and a tight-lipped man who watched the El Paso road with more wariness than curiosity.

Jesse felt no true part of this. But what was he but an aimless wanderer himself, bound for where he knew not, drifting west on instinct alone? At the same time, he was conscious again of the somewhat odd stares he drew. A young man of military carriage whose hair, once fair, grief had turned white overnight in Mexico. Whose worn face and weary gray eyes now belonged to an older-looking man, a much older man. He thought back on his past ruefully. In twenty-eight years of life, almost seven had been spent in war. Three wars, including service on the Plains. He wanted to cry out, *"Enough!"*

A shout sounded, and swinging in off the El Paso road rolled a six-wagon train, its mules stepping briskly and still full of travel. In the lead was a big man wearing a big hat astride a big black Morgan, its neck arched. *A stud-horse man,* Jesse thought, admiring the mount. The mules likewise held his eye, powerful and long-striding, like the ones his mule-man father in Tennessee had raised and sold to cotton farmers in Alabama and Mississippi before the war. The thought disturbed him, broke his calm, taking him back until he blocked it from his mind.

At the rider's stiff-armed signal, the drivers formed a half circle and halted. Whereupon, as if suddenly released, tow-headed children and plain-faced women descended from the wagons and gazed at the village, the shrill young ones scampering like foals in a pasture. Jesse watched with sympathy. *Poor folks gettin' out of the South, left impoverished by the war. A man could understand that.*

The rider on the fine Morgan rode up to the feed store, swung down and went in, spurs jingling, his manner aggressive. In moments, Jesse heard a brassy voice wrangling over prices, overriding the soft, conciliatory tones of the Mexican storekeeper. The rider stalked out and mounted. Jerking the stallion about, he spurred off for the wagons.

"Don't believe that feller's gonna find feed any cheaper on west," a drifter drawled. "Farther you go, higher it gets—if there be any."

Still with time to kill, Jesse strolled back to the plaza. A kind of general store was doing a steady business in ammunition and guns, canteens, shirts, boots, hats and blankets. He bought two hundred shells for the .56-50 Spencer, a purchase in pesos that stirred a nod from the owner.

"I've been told this gun played a big role for the Union in the West," he said.

"Reckon it did," Jesse agreed, thinking of Hoover's Gap and other bloody fields.

When Jesse did not expand on that, the storekeeper said no more, but his eyes left much unasked.

A steady clanging down a side street led Jesse to a needed farrier, where he had both animals reshod.

"You are going long way, *señor?*"

"A long way," Jesse said.

"Go with God, *señor,*" the farrier said in parting.

As Jesse rode back to the plaza, a detachment of ten dusty troopers and a young officer on jaded horses passed through from the west, the enlisted men casting longing glances at the saloon.

Jesse spent the remainder of the afternoon watching his stock graze at the edge of town, while he rested in the shade of a mesquite. Toward dusk, he tied his stock nearby and started for the saloon. He would not have admitted it, but he actually hungered for the sound of voices after the long, solitary ride up from Querétaro. He could hear the raucous buzz of the saloon as he walked. Across the plaza someone lazily strummed a guitar.

A young Mexican girl stood in the doorway of an adobe, her slim shape outlined against the room's dull light, left hand on hip, a comb high in the blue-black hair, silver earrings dangling. The dimness left her face in shadow, in mystery. She said no word and did not need to, for her dark eyes and manner were invitation enough.

He felt the impulse to go in. Instead, he smiled and passed on, thinking, *Under different circumstances . . .*

The saloon was packed along the bar, tobacco smoke as thick as river fog. Jesse bought tequila and found an empty chair against the rear wall. Games were in progress. He recognized one of the afternoon's black broadcloth gamblers. The young cavalry officer was at the bar, in earnest conversation with the rider on the Morgan who had led in the six-wagon train.

After a while, sharp voices pierced the steady babble. Two men at one end of the long bar. One shouted, "I say the proper name for the war is the Civil War. The Union made you Rebs skedaddle—and don't you forget it! Better yet, call it the Great Rebellion That Failed!"

The other took a hitch at his belt, shouting, "It'll always be the War Between the States down South—and don't you blue-bellied, yellow-livered carpetbaggers forget it!"

They went at it then, like two bulls in a pasture, fists thudding. Those along the bar gave them ground, content to watch.

A bartender called, "Juan!" and a huge Mexican who had been standing, arms folded, at the rear, rushed in and broke them apart. Then he hustled them to the door and out. Unruffled, he resumed his post at the rear.

Senseless, Jesse thought. *It's over. Why won't they let it rest?*

He could hear the same two voices resume shouting outside. The shouts reached a shrill peak. Two shots crashed almost together, and another. Two more quick shots. Silence, broken when a horse pounded away.

A man eased to the door and ventured a peek. He froze, staring. He turned back and said, "Looks like the South won this war. Reckon there's an undertaker handy?"

There was a rush outside to see.

Jesse didn't move.

Presently, the crowd began tramping back inside. From their talk he gathered that the undertaker had been summoned. *As senseless,* he thought, *as Hood's massed infantry charges at Franklin against entrenched Yankees with repeating rifles.*

His glass was empty. The nearest opening at the bar was beside the officer, who was listening to the windy wagon train leader.

"I'm mighty pleased to tell you, Lieutenant, that we don't aim to let the grass grow under us 'tween here and Californy. An' we ain't goin' out there as beggars, either." He lowered his voice a trifle. "I carry enough gold in my wagon to buy land for every family when we get thar. We all sold our farms, everything we couldn't move, and lumped what we got all together." He took a swipe at his mouth. "Furthermore, we don't aim to let the Apaches slow us down. I ain't afeared of airy Indian alive, I God, I ain't. Wasn't brought up that way. My father told me, 'Elijah, never back off,' and I never have. Comin' through buffalo country in Texas, some Comanches jumped us." He threw down a slug of whiskey and gave a belching laugh. "Reckon there was considerable mournin' by the squaws when what was left of that war party slunk back to where they came from. They broke, I God, when I knocked two bucks off horses with my ol' Sharps."

His build went with his voice. He looked as thick across the shoulders as he was across the hips, a straight-up-and-down man, built like the trunk of an oak, bull-necked, over six feet tall, of undoubted enormous physical strength. Shaggy dark brows shaded stern gray eyes which reinforced a bearded, craggy face buttressed by a massive jaw. His big-knuckled hand holding the glass was a blunt sledge.

"Were your wagons corralled, Mr. Benedict, when the Comanches charged?" the officer asked courteously. He was a tall, erect young man, in fact, ramrod straight, in command of himself, his evenly cast face attentive, the hazel eyes considerate and bright with interest.

Jesse took him for a West Pointer, not long on the Apache frontier. Not that Jesse had seen many in the Army of Tennessee. But you could tell. There was a certain air about West Pointers. His shoulder straps without a bar marked him as a second lieutenant. Above the crossed brass sabers on his dusty field hat was the number 3 of his regiment in silver and below the sabers the letter B in silver of his troop.

"No," Benedict said. "We's strung out. No time to corral. I figger Apaches will likewise charge on horseback."

"They won't, I must tell you, sir. Apaches like horses and mules when they can steal them. But almost always they attack on foot—when you least expect it. They are fierce, clever adversaries, and they give no quarter."

"We'll be ready, I God. We will."

"How many armed men in your party, Mr. Benedict?"

"Seven—countin' me. All crack shots. Every man has a good rifle. They's three families of us."

"May I ask your home state, sir?"

"Arkansas. Bred and born there. We've seen hard times and good times, mostly hard. Might say it's been cob-rough since the war. The South is broke. Reason we're headed west." He tossed down another whiskey. His voice grew loose. "Why, out in Californy, they claim all you have t'do is throw out a seed, an' next mornin' hit's sprouted, an' the sun shines ever' day, an' the air is always balmy."

The young officer, manifestly understanding a man's hopes, could only smile at the glorification. In a polite voice, he said, "I can well appreciate your desire to make fast time to your destination in California. However, I cannot suggest too strongly that you either ought to wait for another wagon train to add to your strength, or join our escort to Fort Cummings at sunup in the morning. Be sure to fill your water barrels. There will be three other wagons besides yours, all ox-drawn."

Benedict scowled and looked at his glass. "Oxen are slow."

"Yes, but it would not be wise to strike out on your own, Mr. Benedict. I advise against it, absolutely."

Benedict nodded reluctantly. "Reckon you're right, Lieutenant. We'd best join up with you in the mornin'. We'll stick with you long as them heavy-footed oxen don't slow us down too much. The fastest mules in Missouri, bought special fer this trip, are pullin' our wagons."

"Very good, sir. From Fort Cummings there will be another escort as far as Soldier's Farewell. From there, another to Doubtful Canyon, on the Arizona line."

After Benedict had gone, Jesse turned to the officer. "Lieutenant, I couldn't help overhearing your conversation about the need for sticking together on the trail to Fort Cummings. Could you use another gun in the morning when you form the wagon train under escort?"

"Most welcome, sir. Most welcome indeed." His quick smile was boyish and enthusiastic.

Not a day over twenty-two or -three, Jesse guessed, and said, "My name is Jesse Wilder."

"Tom Ayers." He offered a quick, firm hand. "Third cavalry."

"Join me in a drink, Lieutenant?"

"Honored to, Mr. Wilder. Thank you."

With drinks before them, Jesse said, "Mind telling me more of what to expect on west of here?"

"Well, it's some sixty miles to Cummings, following the old Butterfield Trail. All open country—some broken—or to be precise, the Lower Sonoran Zone of desert plains, which at first glance makes a newcomer think of easier, safer traveling. A most foolish and dangerous assumption." He sipped the raw whiskey without change of expression, like a true Army man who could hold his liquor, Jesse noted. "Believe me, it can lull a traveler into boredom and laxness, which can lead to a fatal sense of false security. About halfway is Slocum's Ranch, which is the main source of stock water between Mesilla and Cummings. It's not much . . . tastes like cow tracks, but it's wet. Be a two-day trip to Slocum's with the oxen. Another two from there, if there's no trouble."

"I suppose you put out flankers?" Jesse asked.

"Always." Ayers eyed Jesse keenly, but politely made no comment. "The most dangerous section of the trail is from Slocum's on in, because we're getting closer to Apache haunts in the Mimbres Mountains. I've been out here a year and it's wise, always, to be on the lookout for trouble west of Slocum's. Maybe a little wagon train stripped and burned, the luckless party wiped out, and which never should have left Mesilla. I've found that most immigrants are in one devil of a hurry and loath to take warning. . . . Some wagons out of water and the stock in bad shape. . . . Or a few luckless riders who thought they could get through. Some men think because they ride fast horses, they can make it. If it were just a horse race, they might. What they don't know is that Apaches can set up an ambush in desert country, hiding behind mesquites or creosote bushes. Or dig holes and lie in them until an unsuspecting rider comes by." He grimaced. "We always carry spades for burial purposes as part of our equipment."

"I saw you come into the plaza," Jesse said. "Only ten troopers. A rather small detachment or detail for escort duty."

Again the penetrating look. "True. But all we can spare at Cummings. We're undermanned. Down to a two-troop post. Scarcely a hundred men at times, counting the cooks. Far under that when sick call is big. We send wood-cutting details into the mountains with platoons."

Their glasses were empty.

"I believe it is my turn, Mr. Wilder."

"I'm obliged, Lieutenant."

By now Jesse was conscious of an unexpected and growing ease between them, built on mutual understanding.

"Fortunately," Ayers resumed, "Cummings is a walled adobe fort, the only one in the territory, I've been told. Otherwise, we could be cleaned out. Even so, it's not unusual to find moccasin tracks inside the quadrangle some mornings. We padlock the armory at night."

"Moccasin tracks, you say?"

"Fairly simple for an Apache. Tie a rock on the end of a lariat. Throw the lariat over the wall. When it catches against the parapet, climb up the rope to the top, then drop down. Return in the same manner. Or use the steps to the parapet. Out here, you learn to expect the unexpected."

Jesse nodded. "I learned that in Chihuahua, which is virtually an economic resource for the Apaches. They come when the moon's full, so they can drive horses and mules at night. Although they take plenty of booty, sometimes women and children, they always leave enough so there will be something to come back for the next time."

"Chihuahua?" Ayers said, interested.

Jesse shrugged the question off, and they chatted on awhile in that relaxed vein until, by common assent, they left the saloon and parted company.

Walking to his animals, Jesse neared the adobe where he had seen the Mexican girl. The door was closed, but a shuttered eye of light peered from the one narrow window. As he passed by, he caught the soft tinkle of feminine laughter, mixed with a white man's heavy voice. At another time he might have envied the man his pleasure.

In the haze of a first-quarter moon, he rode to the low-banked river and watered his stock, led them to a grassy little flat, unpacked and unsaddled, put them on picket and fed from nose bags again.

He unrolled a rubber poncho that held two heavy sleeping blankets. Beside his bed, he laid the Spencer and a Blakeslee Quickloader, a leather-covered wood case that held ten tin tubes of seven metallic cartridges each.

He removed the quickly emptied nose bags, came back and pulled off his boots. Using his saddle as a pillow, he stretched out to sleep, in his ears the singing river and the contentment of his animals cropping the short grass. The red horse stopped grazing and raised his head high, his broad blaze a milky white blur.

Jesse, amused, never tired of observing the horse and his wild ways, always watchful, always suspicious, day or night. *My sentinel. Ears pricked, nostrils quivering, staring off into the night, alert to smells and sounds, he hears things I could never catch.*

After some moments, the horse resumed grazing.

Jesse's amusement held. *I'm safe now. All is well.*

El Soldado—the soldier.

Ana had named the coppery gelding, which might flinch at the first crash of nearby musketry, but had never panicked or bolted. A battlefield horse. Ana had woven the red ribbon in his black mane. Probably only once in a lifetime did a man come into possession of such a horse. Pure chance. A horse that had taken him through jubilation as a racehorse, through battle and, finally, wrenching grief.

He lay back and that last day at Querétaro in Juárez's Spartan headquarters stood before him again, eclipsing the starry night glitter. Every piece of the scene was framed in his memory. The citizen president, as inflexible as rock. The black, Zapotec Indian eyes like bits of flint. The sculpted face of a patriot in bronze. The high cheekbones. The prominent nose. The thick-set, solid body hardly more than five feet in height, but which created the impression of a much larger man.

Pieces of the hurried interview flew like darts across his mind's eye. Jesse pleading for the pardon of Maximilian and the two Mexican generals. "It's barbaric, sir, to execute prisoners. Mexico, freed now from foreign intervention, must rise above that as a nation. As bloody as was our American War Between the States, which the Yankees call the Civil War, neither side shot prisoners."

The Indian face unchanged. "They have been found guilty by our courts. Your plea is denied, Citizen General Wilder."

"There's been so much killing, Señor President, that Mexico runs red with blood. I've lost my beloved Indian wife and my best friend in your war. What Mexico needs now, sir, is mercy and forgiveness to build on."

No outburst of executive anger. Instead, the low, inflexible Indian voice saying, "You are dismissed, General Wilder."

The scene faded as it had many times since, never changing, dissolving bit by bit.

By this time Juárez and his staff had made their triumphal entry into Mexico City after an absence of five years. The new Republic was finally restored, the suspended constitution of 1857 in place, paid for by grinding privation and a sea of blood.

Jesse dropped off into troubled sleep.

Without warning, his crafty demons, absent on the long ride northward, returned in all their old frenzy, leaping here and there. . . . He was in the dew-wet April woods of Shiloh, in the gray line sweeping toward the unsuspecting Yankee camps. A roll of musketry, the startled enemy's firing scattered at first, then bracing. Around him boys falling in windrows. Boys killing boys. His boyhood friend, John Hanover, going down. . . . He was at fateful Franklin. How many times had the reckless Hood sent them against the entrenched Yankees? Bloody hand-to-hand fighting around the Carter House. The furious milling there. Bayonets and rifle butts. The hot scent of firing. A fog of powdersmoke. Seeing Jim Lacey and Todd Drake fall, powerless to help them. Hearing his rebel yell in a voice that seemed a stranger's screaming, "Yee—haaa! Yee—haaa—haaa-haa!" as he jabbed and rammed, no time to reload. Until something smashed his head and side and he fell into utter darkness. . . . He was in the barracks of the Yankee prison at Camp Morton. Smelling the unforgettable stink of unwashed bodies and blankets and woodsmoke. A voice calling him. Why, that was little Willie Reed calling him from the lower bunk. Poor, dying Willie, who had ridden with Morgan's men. . . . He was holding Cullen Floyd in his arms while the Juáristas, machetes flashing, stormed the enemy line on the dusty road to Querétaro. Cullen murmuring, "Long way from home, Jesse," and Jesse answering,

"Home is where we are." Cullen, like himself, an expatriate. Cullen always so full of self-mockery, a Mississippi Floyd, suh. . . . He was astride the red horse, flying through the pine-needled forest toward the Juáristas' camp, knowing he was too late when he heard the crackling volley of French rifles. And finding Ana, his Indian Ana, gunned down with the women and children and few guards left to protect the camp, while the main Juárista force was drawn away by a ruse.

He woke in a cold sweat, sat up and held his throbbing head with both hands. *I've got to get a grip on myself.* So much had happened back there, and he was always the survivor, burdened with guilt. Why? Why? Many times he'd asked that and wished otherwise. Now his old nightmares of the war were joined by new ones: Cullen and Ana. Would the past ever let him go? Time had brought little relief, only the will to endure and accept what life had dealt him. Together, he and the red horse had survived.

Gradually he became aware of an approaching subtle sound, the faintest of movements through grass, which he soon recognized, not wishing to interrupt it. It was like a ritual faithfully followed when he camped at night. First it was a presence whose strong body heat he felt and smelled, and then it was gently sniffing his blankets, and next emitting a grassy breath on his hat brim, but not quite on his face, over him a long, white-streaked visage peering down at him.

Jesse hadn't moved. He felt like smiling.

As if assured that all was well here, the red horse turned and drifted away as quietly as he had come. In moments, Jesse heard him busily cropping grass. Later he would lie down to seek his own sleep.

These were good sounds. His tension broken, Jesse slept.

Two

Soon after sunup Lieutenant Ayers began assembling the train and, to Benedict's annoyance, assigned the mule-drawn wagons to follow the oxen.

"We have to proceed at the rate of the slowest wagons, sir," Jesse heard him patiently tell the Arkansawyer. "Your mules, in the lead, would soon move off and leave us, creating a wide gap. It will be best, even more so after Slocum's Ranch, to keep the column closed up so we could corral at short notice."

Benedict took it with grumbling ill-grace. He lined up his wagons in the rear, his forceful voice like a rasp across the stir of creaking wagons, hoofbeats and the shouting at laggard teams.

As Jesse, leading the mule, drew off to wait, yesterday's two talkative prospectors rode in together, their optimistic chatter unabated. Each with rifles in scabbards, each with a burdened mule on halter. Picks and shovels in the packs. The pale-skinned gambler was next, already uncomfortable in the saddle and evidently dreading the discomfort of the trail, aboard a horse which he had likely purchased out of ignorance, a thin, calf-kneed gray that also toed in and was extremely narrow through the withers. If he carried a weapon, it was hidden on his person in the manner of his profession.

A rather rotund man, the likely merchant bound for mining country, showing an easy smile, followed on a dun saddler. Eager for company, he struck up a mostly one-sided conversation with the gambler. Behind them came the taciturn individual who had watched the El Paso road so intently, a kind of wild defiance in his black eyes under the slouch hat. He halted apart from the others, on a chestnut that looked trail-weary carrying a heavy pack. The rider's manner clearly stated that he neither wished nor needed company. A rifle hung alongside his scarred saddle, and he openly wore a handgun. A gunman on the dodge? He could be many things, Jesse mused.

The train swung into motion toward the river.

At that moment, two riders loped up, the one called Gat and his toothy friend Clinch, the latter trailing along like a loose appendage. They passed Jesse without appearing to notice and posted themselves on a flank.

Jesse stiffened, aware of old warning signals. *Instincts,* he thought, *are seldom wrong out here. More trustworthy than mere words or just what the eye sees. I'll hear from the horse thief later. He still wants the horse. He'll jump me when he figures I'll least expect it.* It was a weary feeling.

When the head of the train neared the crossing, Ayers and his troopers trotted in advance to the waiting ferry. The river was running high, but the bank was cut for easy descent. A Mexican in a straw sombrero waved at the lieutenant. They conversed briefly. Nodding, Ayers rode back to the oxen drivers. "It's fifty cents a wagon," he called out.

"That's high," a man drawled.

"I know it seems so. But it's the only way you can get safely across. River's up from summer rains."

"It don't look too high to me," the driver said.

"It's up two feet and rising. Very swift. You'd better take the ferry, sir, for safety."

"Reckon we'll have to."

The driver urged the oxen down the bank to the ferry, which was attached to the long ropes leading to two teams of mules on the opposite bank and to two teams on this side for the return trip.

A second ox wagon was moving safely across when Benedict rode up with his wagons. Told what the toll was, he roared, "I God, I won't pay that! Narrow as the river is, no reason why a man can't cross his own wagon."

The patient Ayers said, "The narrow banks make for a swifter current. Be safer to take the ferry, Mr. Bendict, I assure you."

"No, we'll cross on our own." Benedict waved at the boy driving his wagon. "Come on, Lafe."

Lafe hesitated.

"I said, come on."

The boy chirruped to the mules. When their hybrid judgment made them balk at the rushing waters, he laid on the leather and the team, with a headlong suddenness, plunged into the river.

For a rod or so, they made progress.

It happened unexpectedly. A mule slipped, thrashing for footing, and the stalled wagon took the full force of the current. Lafe shouted in alarm. So did the family behind him. The wagon started to roll.

Ayers shouted at his men and they dashed after him into the rising waters, Benedict following.

Ayers grabbed a struggling mule's bridle, a trooper the other mule's bridle, while others steadied the wagon amid a chorus of screaming kids and a woman. Ayers righted his mule, got him headed again, slowly breasting the tugging current. Suddenly they reached the bank. An instant's pause, and then mules and blue-clad troopers, mud and water flying, went scrambling upward to firm ground.

After a word with Ayers, Benedict, chagrined, put the powerful black stud back into the water, crossed without difficulty, and started lining up his wagons at the crossing.

When all the wagons had crossed, Jesse, joined by the gambler and the merchant and the prospectors, paid the ferryman a peso and rode aboard to keep his supplies and camping gear dry. The other riders swam their horses across.

The train assembled again, the lieutenant set a course across the bottom lands toward the foothills of a broad mesa and a distant cone-shaped peak.

Seeing Jesse riding as a flanker, Ayers waved him to the head of the column. "You might as well ride up here, Mr. Wilder, if you don't mind."

"Glad to have the company, Lieutenant. I'm obliged."

Ayers's eyes noticed at once the sheathed carbine and the Quickloader, tied on a leather strap to the saddle horn. "I believe you're carrying a Spencer carbine repeater. We could use the same out here. We're equipped with a single-shot .50-70 Government Springfield."

"It's a good gun," Jesse said. "Beats the old muzzleloaders a country mile."

"What Spencer model is yours, sir?"

"Came out in 'sixty-five, the .56-50. What they call the Indian Model. The 'sixty-three Spencer rifles were either .56-50s, or .56-52s."

"Tell me about your Spencer. I've never handled one."

"It holds seven cartridges in the magazine. Insert one in the chamber and you've got an eight-shooter. You ear back the hammer for each shot."

"And the leather-covered case, I presume, is the celebrated Quickloader I've heard about?"

"The Blakeslee Quickloader. Mine holds ten tubes. Some hold thirteen. The sling goes over the shoulder. You withdraw the empty magazine from the butt stock, slide in the cartridges from a tube, put the tube back, reinsert the magazine and lock the cover plate. The magazine is spring-loaded—that keeps the cartridges pushed forward. After firing, the trigger guard is lowered to eject the empty case and bring up a new one. Gives a sustained fire of fourteen to sixteen shots a minute." Jesse paused. "But keep that up very long and the barrel can get too hot to hold. Depending on the situation."

"But it's such an advantage against muzzle-loaders firing two to three rounds a minute."

"This gun does have one dangerous whim," Jesse said, smiling. "Bang the butt hard on the ground when fully loaded and it can go off, with disastrous results for the holder."

"How do you avoid that?"

"I'm careful not to bang it. No reason to, generally. Most times I carry it with only one shell in the chamber. I keep it handy, the way most men pack six-shooters."

"The sight of it should discourage trouble."

As the morning wore away, the train seemed to crawl like a tired snake over the long slopes of the mesa's barren foothills. By the time they reached the landmark peak, the brilliant sun stood high. Ayers halted to rest the teams. Within half an hour, he led off northwest, climbing through a pass, and after more toilsome miles gained the summit of the mesa, where he ordered another halt and dismounted.

Benedict dashed up, the black Morgan fighting the bit. "What's the holdup, Lieutenant?"

"Teams need to rest, Mr. Benedict. Even your mules. These long pulls take a good deal out of an animal. We've been going uphill ever since we left the bottoms."

"Where you aim to make camp tonight?"

"At the old relay station in the Rough-and-Ready Hills. Approximately fourteen miles. It'll look inviting after what we've had today."

By no means appeased, Benedict scowled and whirled the stud and left on the run. At the wagons he pulled up to converse with Gat.

"That man Benedict's talking to," Jesse said, watching. "I heard him called Gat back in Mesilla. Do you know anything about him?"

"I've noticed him several times in trains making up at Mesilla for Cummings. I believe his name is Gat Shell, though we've never spoken. What I'd call a floater. Frontier type. Drifts here and there. May trade a little. My main thinking is that he hires on as a guard sometimes—gets by that way."

"He also may *trade* in horses," Jesse said, with emphasis. "He tried to steal my horse yesterday afternoon in Mesilla while I was in the saloon."

"The devil you say!"

"I heard a ruckus, the crowd yelling, and ran outside. My horse had thrown him. He was going to try to mount again when I stood him off with the carbine. A common horse thief, no more."

"He would have left you on foot."

"Not likely. This horse ran wild for a number of years. I bought him as a five-year-old out of a bunch of trader's horses in El Paso. Believe me, it took a while before he settled down. He'd never had a saddle on him. He threw me again and again. He won't let strangers ride him. He was tied, or Gat Shell could never have mounted."

"I like his spirit."

"We've been through a great deal together," Jesse said, and checked himself. Was he talking too much? Or did it matter? If so, it was understandable. Ayers was the first sociable person he'd met since leaving Querétaro.

Ayers's attention, still on the red horse, held outright approval. "Out here a good horse often means the difference between life and death. Your mount had caught my eye earlier. Nice head. A good, short back. Long barrel. Sloping shoulder, which means speed and a long stride. Straight legs. Well-muscled hindquarters. Short cannons and pasterns. Not a big horse, but big enough. Compact. Well-balanced."

"I believe you know more than just a little bit about horses," Jesse said, impressed.

"I grew up in Kentucky."

Ayers stepped to the saddle. "Time to get along. No doubt friend Benedict is champing at the bit, cursing a mere second lieutenant for delaying his arrival in Elysium."

Travel became much easier now. In the distance, flankers bobbed like corks on the sea of short grass while the train crawled toward the spur of a great thrust of mountains.

Ayers said, "If there's one thing service does in Apache country, it just about eliminates straggling. A trooper who lags very far behind can end up dead."

"Even in open country like this?" Jesse said.

"Even in open country. They can spot our dust from the mountains and set up something. Nor do we have many desertions at Cummings. No nearby towns where a trooper can go lose himself. In my time out here, only two have tried it. We found their bodies along the Mesilla trail. Hacked and stripped to the last thread of clothing. Boots gone. Poor fellows."

"Fighting Apaches is far different from fighting Plains Indians," Jesse said. "On the Plains, they fight from horseback, like light cavalry, dashing in and out, whooping all the while. Or at a distance, they make insulting signs and challenge you to come out and fight singlehanded. If you don't, they sign that you're a woman. Bravery is the most important object of their free-roving lives. By contrast, in Chihuahua, the Apaches fight on foot—as you told Benedict—striking at first light out of the east, when the sun is in your eyes, or jumping your outfit from ambush as you're crossing a deep wash. They hate all white people, and Mexicans with a particular passion, which is returned in full."

Nodding, Ayers asked politely, "In Chihuahua?"

"In Chihuahua," Jesse said, his voice trailing off. Would his life be long enough for him to get over the past, not only in Chihuahua, but in the war as well?

Ayers did not press the question. His good manners forbade that.

Back in Tennessee during his sunny years as a boy, Jesse remembered an elderly aunt who lived with the family saying, "Time heals all things—it just takes a heap of it." *Time,* he thought, *is more like a scarring over, leaving the hurt underneath. Yet grief is linked to our love, and if we did not mourn, there would have been no love back there. What man would want to forget people he'd loved?*

The reflection had come to him very suddenly. He let it float in his mind, finding unexpected consolation.

The afternoon slipped by, the red horse still as eager to travel as he was at daybreak, Jesse having to rein him in at times from his customary running walk. At intervals, Jesse pulled out with Ayers to see how the trailing wagons fared. Shell and Benedict rode together, Clinch in the rear. Apparently, they found plenty to talk about. *Shell's sold himself as a needed hand,* Jesse thought. *Might go on to California, he says. Don't you believe it, Benedict, and keep an eye on your fine Morgan stud. Some morning soon the stud and Shell may be long gone.*

The merchant and the gambler also rode side by side. The miners likewise, often pointing northwest toward the promise of the mountains. The tight-lipped man on the chestnut rode alone, but he still eyed the back trail now and then. In a fight, Jesse judged, he might be the most reliable of the bunch.

Just when there seemed no end to this section of the trail, and the afternoon was dying, Ayers entered a gap in a range of hills and Jesse saw the remains of a roofless stage station, part stone, part adobe, an adobe corral abutting it. Close by an earthen-made tank held water.

He watered his stock, unpacked and unsaddled on the far side of the station and picketed for the night. Behind him he heard the bedlam of drivers taking horses, mules and oxen to water, and the chatter of families welcoming the respite from the wearying day. As he went about his early camping duties, unrolling the poncho and taking kindling from a pack for a little supper fire, the red horse and the mule regarded him impatiently, watching each movement with an anticipation that evoked his smile.

"Well, all right," he teased them. "All right. Guess I'll have to feed you."

He was feeding from nose bags when the lieutenant rode up.

"I see you look after your stock," he said.

"Just a few handfuls of oats and bran in the evening, when we're on the move. I'll run out before long. Helps them to know that I'm looking out for them."

"A good idea out here. Might keep stock close to camp if they happened to break picket. Came over to tell you that you're invited to supper with the escort, if you can stand cavalry field rations."

"I haven't forgotten. Sounds good to me. I'm obliged. Later, I hope you can have a drink with me."

"A man never turns down a drink in arid country."

"I'll hold you to that, Lieutenant."

After a time, his two friends having finished their modest rations, he removed the nose bags and laid them by the packs. The noisy encampment drew his attention. The troopers had set picket lines. Their supper fires blazed like yellow tongues licking the last of the fading light. Benedict had taken over the stage station for his people, blocking any passage from the oxen wagons, a strong suggestion that the long-striding mules take the lead tomorrow.

A vague unease brushed Jesse. From the rim of his eye he saw that he was being observed. A man standing by the first mule wagon. Gat Shell. Jesse's glance met Shell's, remained there until Shell stirred and drifted back among the wagons. *So it's not over yet. Before long he'll make another play, unless he takes the Morgan stud first. Well, we'll see. . . .*

Presently, taking tin plate, tin cup, knife and fork, Jesse crossed to the escort's camp. Supper, as he expected from the past, did not deviate from the usual Union cavalry fare of hardtack, bacon and bitterly black coffee, just what a man needed on the march. The troopers were mainly Irish, tough, dependable fighters, as he also remembered, mixed sometimes with Southerners, men steeped in centuries-old superstitions, like the Evil Eye.

When supper was over, Jesse visited a proper time, then speaking his thanks, he nodded to the men and returned to camp. Ayers joined him not long after.

"This tequila is much better than the whiskey I had in Mesilla," Ayers said, handing back the bottle.

"Glad you like it."

They sat awhile in silence. The sky darkened and a grass-scented wind, cool and damp, rolled through the gap, hinting of more rainy-season showers in the offing. Maybe so tonight, maybe not.

In a conversational tone that reminded Jesse of other nights and other bivouacs, Ayers said, "I believe you're a man of considerable military experience, which the escort may need before we reach Fort Cummings."

"Hope not."

"And without prying into your past, Mr. Wilder, which I have no desire to do, your accent tells me your services weren't in the North."

"You're correct about the first, but only half right on the second."

"Oh?" Ayers said, both respectful and waiting.

Jesse took a swallow, then passed the bottle. "I was a captain in General Cheatham's division, the Army of Tennessee, General Hood commanding."

"Ah, the Army of Tennessee and the gallant Hood."

"Rather, the damn-fool Hood, Lieutenant. We lost some six thousand men at Franklin in senseless charges against entrenched veterans, some Union battalions armed with Spencer repeating rifles. Oh, we made a gallant sight, sir, when we lined up the first time that late November afternoon, flags fluttering in the breeze." Jesse's bitterness hadn't diminished, but he felt relieved to talk about it. There'd been few listeners in Mexico.

"I read and heard a good deal about the battle in military history at West Point."

"Did the books or the professor tell you that Hood was so wrathy and impatient to get at the Yankees that he wouldn't wait for his artillery to come up?"

"Not that I recall."

"He didn't, and it was slaughter. Not just once, but time after time we charged. Still hell-bent on self-destruction, apparently, he followed the Yankees on up to Nashville, where he managed to get the Army of Tennessee virtually destroyed as a fighting force the rest of the war. My own service ended at Franklin." He paused, feeling uncomfortable. "I'm talking too much, besides maybe boring you."

"Not at all, Captain. I wish you would continue."

"Wounded at Franklin, I ended up, by mistake, in a Yankee hospital in Nashville. A mistake that probably saved my life, because I got good care, which surprised me, bein' a Reb. When I recovered, I was given a choice: go to prison camp or volunteer for the Union Army on the western frontier. Wear the hated Yankee blue? Why, I'd feel like a Judas. . . . At Camp Morton, Indiana, I faced the choice again. Eventually starve or die of disease, or else volunteer. Three of us tried to escape. We didn't make it. My two friends died, shot down in the prison yard. We'd been led into a trap." He fell silent again, reliving it all. "A few days later I took the oath of allegiance to the Union, feeling like the most contemptible traitor possible to the South and my friends. So I wore the blue out West. Fought Plains Indians . . . served in escorts protecting supply trains and stages . . . post duty . . . everything. There were a good number of us so-called galvanized Yankees." He thought it unnecessary to relate what happened after he was mustered out and returned home: neighbors not only turning their backs, but his father disinheriting him as well. That was a family matter, though he had no family anymore, and a man didn't talk about family matters.

A thoughtful silence settled between them, broken when Jesse passed the bottle again.

"I think," he said, "it's time to put the war behind us. To let it rest in peace. But due to man's cussedness, its sleep will be troubled for years. We saw that when a man was shot to death outside the saloon in Mesilla simply over what to call the war. How senseless! Just another wasted life."

"What would you call the war, Captain?"

"Nothing high-sounding or grandiose, I assure you. I'd call it what it really was—the Fratricide War. I believe that's when brother kills brother. In prison, I heard Rebs call it a rich man's war, a poor man's fight. Wealthy draftees could pay substitutes to serve in their place. A man with twenty slaves didn't have to serve."

Thoughtfully, Ayers asked, "What combination of forces do you think brought on the final explosion? What actually set it off, brought it to an emotional boil, leaving aside the attack on Fort Sumter?"

"Looking back, I reckon it had been sputtering for years, like a damp fuse. I grew up on a farm, but I went to school and read books and Southern newspapers. . . . Slavery was at the heart of the war, but a big part of it was economic. The South felt it was being treated like an economic vassal by the commercial and industrial interests of the North—I remember reading that. Mighty puffed-up talk. And unequal tariff laws. And the argument over states' rights. . . . Seems like everything forced the South to extremes—secession and defending slavery. . . . But the match that set off the powder keg, I think, was struck by the Southern fire-eaters. Why, they'd foam at the mouth when you mentioned black Republicans. I saw that happen back home more than once. They knew how to start a war, but they didn't know how to stop it."

"Did the war have to happen?"

"I don't think it had to, but it was inevitable, yes. Passions got so high, and reason was so ignored. Besides the fire-eaters, there were the equally bull-headed abolitionists, and there was oversensitive Southern pride, and Southern honor, sir, of which there is nothing quite so touchy. . . . The influence of the planter class had to be broken. You see, most of the Johnny Rebs owned no slaves. The planters and fire-eaters and Southern pride got us into it."

"What did you do before the war, Captain?"

"I was a country school teacher. My father raised and sold cotton mules. Although he'd freed his slaves several years before the war, he hated the North. Particularly Northern bankers. Called 'em leeches."

"I venture that you volunteered, Captain?"

"I couldn't wait to get in with my friends. All of us afraid the fighting would be over before we could fire a shot. When the band played 'Dixie' and the girls waved, a boy felt he could whip ten Yankees any day, and twice on Sunday."

Ayers came to his feet and held out a hand. "Enjoyed the drinks and the soldierly chat. . . . By the way, my father, Colonel Jonathan Ayers, died at Franklin."

Startled, Jesse grasped his hand harder. "My God, I'm sorry—most sorry. You have my heartfelt sympathy, Lieutenant. I hate to hear that."

"Thank you, Captain. At least you and I can let the war rest in peace—that is something," he said, and lost himself in the gathering desert darkness.

Jesse, watching, was moved and the feeling stayed with him until he slept.

Three

Breaking camp early next morning, Jesse started to mount. At once the red horse danced away, flung up his blazed head and blew through his nostrils.

Jesse had to chuckle at the show of independence. "Every now and then," he said, "you have to remind me that you used to run wild. Well, I haven't forgotten that, but don't you forget that I'm still in command."

As he reached for the saddlehorn again, the horse danced away as before. "That's enough—you've made your point. Now settle down." This time, he shortened his hold on the open reins, moved faster and mounted, braced for some bucking. But nothing happened. This act, Jesse thought, was becoming an established ritual at the start of day when a horse felt his oats, not unlike a favorite little game between them. Whatever, it was enough to make a man smile when not in a hurry. So far the red horse had not tried it when danger threatened.

The mule wagons, Benedict in the lead, left the gap and were rolling on down the rutted trail after the escort when Ayers raised a halting hand.

"We follow the same order as before, Mr. Benedict," Ayers said firmly, but pleasantly. "The ox wagons will take the lead."

"I can't stomach this snail's pace, young sir."

"It's for the safety of everyone, sir."

"So you say, but we're able to look out for ourselves."

"I understand how you feel, sir, but I cannot agree with you under the circumstances. We'll proceed as before."

Grudgingly, Benedict held up until the ox-drawn wagons lumbered by into the lead.

The beady sun soon took over and the morning turned hot and dusty. Riding alongside Ayers, Jesse reflected that last night he had said more than he'd intended; tequila and a good companion, a soldier who was also a dead soldier's son, had opened a curtain on his past. But Mexico's grip was still hard upon him, still too keenly felt to talk about. It rode with him now, this instant, still fresh: faces like cameos, events, moments, fragments, smells, flashes of action, especially the faces. Yet there'd been time for laughter as well, time for love. He saw again her high-boned face, her skin the color of earth, felt the giving of her lovely young body, heard her soft voice.

So again, forcibly, he closed his mind against it and any self-pity, a weakness he despised. It was his to bear, his to distance himself from, unless he wished to consume himself by brooding. In that connection, he felt a kinship with the troopers, their taxing duty and low pay, their drinking, when they could get it, their fights over women, and what they had left behind them in the Old Sod, now best put aside.

Somewhere near eleven o'clock the column came upon five headboard grave markers, the blackened debris of two burned wagons, and the skeletal remains of mules.

"This happened last fall," Ayers said, halting the wagons. "A family headed for what they no doubt thought was the riches of the gold and silver mines around Pinos Altos. Missouri people. Farmers. I hope this will serve to remind Benedict what can happen when a small train strikes out on its own."

"I doubt if even this will change his mind," Jesse said. "He's a bull-headed man, his opinions set in stone. He sees all Indians as being alike, which is a dangerous miscalculation. Thinks Apaches will attack on horseback, in the open like Comanches."

"I'm afraid you're right. Well, if he breaks loose, there's nothing I can do about it. . . . It's believed that Ramos did this."

"Ramos?"

"Ramos, the shadowy raider. The story is that he's a Mexican stolen as a child by Apaches and brought up as an Indian. You hear a lot of wild stories." Ayers signaled for the train to move on. "We've seen enough of this."

"Maybe this Ramos is more myth than fact."

"But the name persists and so do the attacks, but always on a small train traveling without escort, always marked by the most thorough looting you could ever imagine, down to the last detail. Every piece of clothing taken—the bodies stripped. This train was picked clean. Even of cutlery, dishes, coffee pots, buckets. Even shoes and boots. Even baby clothes. Everything . . . whatever might be of use, including chairs and tables, because we found none. Nothing left. Harness taken from horses and mules. What couldn't be taken, burned."

"How do they haul it off?"

"Would you believe, in wagons from the train? That, and they must have pack mules. All very simple and organized, I'd say. I saw firsthand evidence of that here, and I hope to God I never do again. It's been a very fast growing up for me, Captain, coming from a theoretical, textbook world."

"Yet, I can't see Apache warriors driving wagons."

"Mexicans could, and Apaches could learn."

"If they haven't attacked escorted trains, they must know in advance what's coming."

"Not necessarily. Look at the dust we're kicking up now. On a clear day, from the mountains, I should think a train could be spotted many miles away through field glasses."

"Has anyone ever trailed the tracks of the loot wagons?"

"Not to my knowledge. My own detachment, like this one, was too small that day here to split up and follow old tracks and risk leaving the train with a few troopers. All we could do was bury the dead. But you can be sure that the wagon tracks headed off toward the Mimbres Mountains, not Mexico. We saw that. So did the tracks from the earlier ambushes, they say."

"Tell me about the Mimbres Mountains. My geography is blank on southern New Mexico."

"The mountains end near Fort Cummings. Cooke's Peak, which you can see now—that highest peak—is the principal landmark. Named after Colonel St. George Cooke, who led the Mormon Battalion from Santa Fe to California in 1846 and broke trail for much of the wagon road that eventually became the Butterfield. On north, beyond the Mimbres range, rises the Black Range. In all that, there's no rougher country in the world for cavalry."

"I can see the obstacles to pursuit, Lieutenant."

"I said a train under escort had never been attacked. But wood-cutting details from the post have, and couriers have been killed between Cummings and Fort Selden, over on the Rio Grande. We know the post is constantly watched. It's not unusual to see figures in the foothills, horseback or on foot."

Their talk ended when Ayers rode out to speak to a flanking trooper. Glancing idly about, Jesse saw Shell riding as usual with Benedict. At this short distance, he could make out Shell's features, which seemed fixed and unrelenting, the embodiment, he thought, of a border hardcase, the eyes never wavering from Jesse's. Turning away, Jesse sensed an inevitable conclusion before the train reached the post.

After the noon rest, lassitude seemed to settle over the train plodding across the greening mesquite. In the far distance, Cooke's Peak, hooking into the sky, appeared tantalizingly near, a fooling impression, Jesse knew, in this clear, arid air.

Suddenly, as if in exasperation, Benedict came spurring by the lead riders and dashed out a way, wheeled the black stud and raced back, not pausing to speak or nod to the lieutenant.

"I take it," Ayers said, grinning, "he's somewhat miffed at our slow but certain progress."

It seemed a long time before Slocum's Ranch materialized under the shuttered eye of the lowering sun: a low, rambling adobe with a watch tower on top, a veranda running the length of the house, three dug water tanks, two large adobe corrals, and a cluster of stables and parked wagons.

A man on a gray mule rode out to meet them.

"Here comes the proprietor himself," Ayers said. "John Slocum.

A fearless entrepreneur if there ever was one. Imagine a man running a stage stop and hotel in the heart of Apache country. He ranches on the side. When the Apaches get hungry, they run off some beeves, or a horse or mule that's strayed. They seem to favor horse meat, he says—his best saddlers, of course. In dry times, he hauls water from the Rio Grande. He trades some. Will buy a lame animal off an immigrant, rest it, feed it, then sell it to the next needy traveler. You'll find him cordial and informative. Under his geniality, however, is a tough and capable frontiersman. He's had several close scrapes with Apaches. His ranch serves as a listening post. News from all around. Mexicans working for him hear things Anglos don't. Bits of information from the border and the mountains. Whispers, you might say. Voices on the wind telling about Ramos."

"Mighty glad to see you again, Lieutenant," Slocum said, shaking hands. "No charge for water this time of year durin' the rainy season. I remind you again of my well-supplied tables, served with all the grace of the Hispanic Southwest. Dinner just two-bits, American. Or a peso will do. All you can eat. Antelope steak tonight, no less. With biscuits, gravy, beans and cornbread. . . . But sorry, no sugar in the cornbread, Yankee style. I have a sense of honor, sir. . . . Not forgetting the many refinements of my saloon, where I serve the best whiskey between Fort Cummings and the Rio Grande, bar none, and every man is treated like a gentleman, whether he is or not, unless he becomes not."

"You mean you serve the only whiskey sold between Cummings and the river, good or bad," Ayers bantered. He introduced the two men.

Jesse, shaking hands, saw a gangling man in about his early fifties. He was thin and straight, his grayish beard like thick moss over an open, friendly face and slate-gray eyes that looked straight at you. A driving force flowed out of him, a restless energy.

"Never mind what this here lieutenant says," Slocum said. "But I never serve whiskey that I won't drink myself, and I never water down whiskey I sell—which, next to murder and horse stealing, is the lowest crime there is out here, in my opinion. Now, Mr. Wilder, you and officer Tom come by tonight and have a drink on the house."

He rode on. Soon, Jesse heard his genial voice at the ox wagons.

Perhaps it was the sight of the solitary house way out here in this great, limitless world, and its reminder of the civilization they'd left behind, and the big black-and-yellow dog barking at the oxen and mules, a clamor soon replaced by much tail-wagging, and the friendly Mexicans smiling welcome from the long veranda. Because as soon as the wagons were corraled and while the men led the teams to the water tanks, the families seemed content just to stroll and look about before fixing supper.

Jesse watered his stock, made camp not far from the ox wagons and fed from the nose bags. Tonight he would dine at Slocum's festive board, after a stop in the saloon. The sky was darkening; a cool wind rose off the desert. He started to leave his carbine in his pack, but decided otherwise and took it along, carrying it inconspicuously, barrel down at his left side. Old and wary habits were hard to break.

Entering the dirt-floor saloon, Jesse smiled inwardly when he saw Slocum's "many refinements." The bar was two rough planks nailed across three rotund whiskey barrels. Slocum was the bartender. Behind him, on a tier of smaller whiskey barrels, stood a row of murky glasses and whiskey bottles. Four rough tables sat aslant on the uneven floor, with plain, stout chairs of dark wood and carved arms showing their Mexican derivation, probably hauled in from El Paso. Greenish-yellow light from hanging lanterns lent the place an air of refuge from the outer world.

The two miners occupied one table, the merchant and the gambler another, the former leading the conversation, the other a pained and trapped listener. Benedict was filling Slocum's ear. Shell's gap-toothed companion, also at the bar, grinned vapidly over a glass. At the farthest table where he could watch the door sat the lone individual. Jesse saw all these pieces, but there was one missing. Where was Shell?

Jesse went to the bar and asked for tequila.

"I'm out, but the whiskey's not bad."

It wasn't.

Ayers joined him and had whiskey.

Seeing Ayers, Benedict moved in next to him. "Lieutenant, them oxen do wear on my patience. They don't walk, they crawl. Must be part snake or turtle. A plumb different breed of oxen from what we're used to in Arkansas."

"I realize it's slow, Mr. Benedict, but it's safer for the train to stick together."

"And so far not one sign of Apaches."

Ayers straightened a little. "Just the five headboards, Mr. Benedict. And the burned wagons, and the remains of the mules. Those were Missouri mules, I've been told."

"That was an old fight."

"Not so old it can't happen again."

Very much full of himself, Benedict turned to Slocum. "What d'you hear on the trail?"

Slocum smiled. "Well, folks don't exactly come in here every day bustin' out with news. But a few days ago a party of miners, headed east with fair stakes, all goin' home by way of Fort Selden, said they saw mounted Indians twice."

"But they didn't attack?"

"Nope."

"How many miners in the party?"

"Ten. All well armed with repeating rifles, well mounted, well organized, travelin' fast."

Benedict gave the plank bar a glass-rattling thump and jogged his I-told-you-so look around. "Jest like I been sayin', I God! No gut-eatin' Indian's gonna jump you if you put up a bold front and let 'em know you mean business. They're all cowards at heart, afraid to face a white man."

Slocum's head snapped up, his bearded mouth shaping protest. "I have to disagree with you there, my friend. A 'Pache has to fight a different war from a white man. Since there's not many of 'em, they can't afford to bunch up and make them fool suicide charges like both sides did durin' the war till the dead lay in windrows. So they slip in and jump you when you least expect it. They're sly and they're cruel. But they're not cowards. In a hand-to-hand fight, no man is braver or tougher to beat. Personally, I'd rather fight a white man in close any day than a 'Pache."

"But them miners got through without airy a shot bein' fired at 'em, you say?"

"They did to here—but they never made camp after leavin' Fort Cummings. Rode straight through to the ranch. Didn't even stop at the old Goodsight Stage Station. Just halted now and then to rest their horses and pack mules."

"Proves it can be done."

"Maybe they had some luck, too. Maybe a heap of it. 'Paches don't hit everything that moves on the trail. Sometimes a few months'll go by without trouble. Why attack a well-armed outfit or one under military escort? Why not wait for some easy pickin's?"

"What do you call easy pickin's?"

"Say a little bunch of riders, or a few wagons without escort."

"Appears to me, Slocum, the Apaches have got all you folks along the trail plumb buffaloed."

"If that means stayin' alive, then we're buffaloed," Slocum said, his grin mirthless.

Benedict let the matter rest. He downed his drink and strode out.

"There," observed Slocum, "goes a man who takes good advice about as far as water soaks into a duck's back. If it was daylight, I'd show him the little cemetery I've set aside north of the ranch for folks who've been killed on the trail. I call it Pilgrim's Rest. Got a nice little juniper fence around it. In it some fellers just like him. I'm tired talkin' to greenhorn know-it-alls. Why don't you boys have that drink on the house? It's the same stuff I drink myself."

He turned, his invitation including Shell's partner, but Clinch had gone.

Slocum talked on, citing prospects for trade at Pinos Altos. "Man could make a fortune if he could get his merchandise through. If he got bushwhacked on the way, he could also lose a fortune, along with his life. Believe, for now, I'll be content just to stay here and make an ordinary living. Just sit on the porch while I watch the pilgrims pass by. I figure I'm about on the edge of what the 'Paches might call their territory. I'm not greedy. I sure don't want to encroach."

Ayers finished his drink, thanked his host and, declining Jesse's invitation to dinner, left for the bivouac.

Supper, Jesse found, included not only Slocum's promised antelope steaks swimming in gravy, and beans, biscuits, and non-Yankee cornbread, but vegetables from the ranch garden. Shy Mexican girls served the long tables amid swarms of circling flies.

Afterward, from the long veranda, he watched the campfires burning against the purple shadows. He caught the fading, pleasant hum of tired voices as the families prepared for bed. He hunched his shoulders against the wanderlust wind prowling off the desert plains, feeling a fresh contentment and anticipation of what tomorrow might bring. In Tennessee he had pictured the desert as a land of only sand and cactus, lizards and snakes. Indeed a misconception. Instead, there was much promise here. An empire of grass awaiting the hardy cattleman. Freighting and various lines of business ventures supplying mankind's many needs on the changing frontier.

A man with determination and a little capital could make it here. Riding out of Mexico, he had thought this several times. But at that point his enthusiasm always seemed to ebb. His schoolteaching aside, interrupted by the war, his only true profession was war. He was good at it. He was damned good at it, was Jesse Alden Wilder, who'd done a heap of killing and maneuvering. Any man was good at it who'd fought through the three-day horror in the Shiloh woods, up into Kentucky and down through Georgia to Atlanta, and on to bloody Franklin in late 'sixty-four. Who'd also learned from the fast-hitting, light cavalry tactics of the superbly mounted Comanches, Sioux and Cheyenne. Who, with Cullen Floyd, could take Mexican peasants, fresh from their bean and chili and corn patches, and forge them into tough fighters, training them to fight in formation and obey officers, using muzzle loaders and Spencer repeaters. Peasant patriots who'd defeated the veteran French Foreign Legion at San Juan de Río and Presdio Montaña and won a dozen savage skirmishes. A man who'd fought *bandidos* and Apaches in Mexico as well. Later, after Ana's death, when Juárez had had made Jesse a citizen general, the patriots called him *El Soldado del Pelo Blanco,* the Soldier of the White Hair.

Three wars, Jesse thought. Some people might call him a mercenary. But he hadn't fought for pay. Twice he'd fought from the heart for what he thought just, first for his home, his state, the South, the second time to help poor peasants throw off the shackles of foreign domination. In the words of Cullen, "One war we won." The third, in the West, he wore the hated blue so he could survive.

He did not forget the greatest, wisest and kindest man he'd ever known or expected to know—Father Alberto Garza, stripped of all priestly privileges by the church because he had sided with the poor Juáristas and President Juárez. An unimpressive little man at first glance, who without prior military training had gathered a few hundred peons he called "my boys," hoping to make them into an army. Father Alberto had virtually given Jesse back his life after he'd lost everything. His hand was on Jesse's head while he murmured, "I felt the same bitterness as yours when Apaches killed my dear mother and father . . . my dear brothers and my precious little sister—my entire family. One day a happy family, the next day wiped out. Man's cruelty to man. But God understood my grief. He touched me as he is touching you now through me . . . in love and understanding, which you will feel, I promise you. He will dry your tears. He will raise you up. He will not forsake you. He cannot heal the hurt but he can take away some of the pain."

And at Querétaro, when the fighting was over:

"This brings us to the end, doesn't it, *amigo?* Tomorrow I shall disband our tough little army, send the boys back to their little patches of land with hopes for the future. The raw boys you and Cullen so generously and nobly trained and made into soldiers, proving that victories demand more than passion . . . But you don't have to leave. Mexico has a home for you. I will find one for you."

And when Jesse had demurred, saying he felt he should return to the states: "You have finished what you and Cullen set out to do. Mexico will not forget. You can always come back to us."

And that last day at Querétaro, after Juárez had turned down Jesse's pleas: "I know you will find peace of mind somewhere, *amigo* Jesse, because you believe in God, and God always provides in some way. . . . *Un abrazo, amigo.*"

The scenes faded. It was good to remember good people, but it wasn't good to let the mind stray back too much, to dwell on the past.

Thinking of his stock, he went out to his camp beyond the wagons and left the carbine beside his bedroll. Both picket pins were firmly in place. The mule, busy grazing, ignored him, but the red horse swung around and warily lifted his head and watched him, making a snuffling rattle through his nostrils.

Jesse all but laughed. *Ever playing the wild horse, aren't you, my wary friend? You can smell me. You know who I am. You trust me. But damned if you'll come up for me to pet you. You never will. Only at night, when you're making your rounds on sentry duty, will you approach me. Then it's strictly in the line of duty, sir. Just walking your post like a good soldier.*

Chuckling, Jesse moved to him, stroked the blazed face and rubbed behind the flicking ears. There was no backing away.

He was going back to his bedroll when bit by bit, then suddenly, he sensed a nearby wrongness of sound. The next he knew was a rushing movement behind him. Before he could turn, a blow across his shoulders sent him reeling to the ground. And before he could get up, he felt a savage kick to his left thigh. He rolled away and was rising to stand when the man rushed him. Jesse felt a rain of blows across his chest and face.

The man muttered, "Forgot to pack your carbine this time, red horseman."

Gat Shell. Who else?

Jesse's head cleared. He would not waste time talking. He swung right-handed for Shell's face. Shell ducked away, but Jesse followed up with a hook to the ribs. It was like hitting a side of beef, that solid. Still, the blow drew a deep grunt. In the manner of a barroom fighter, Shell attacked at a crouch, closed with a flurry of blows. His power was astonishing. Jesse went down. But as Shell started to leap upon him, Jesse kicked with both feet and felt his boots strike ribs and belly. Shell grunted and staggered back, winded, but not down. In that pause, Jesse leaped up and charged, swinging for Shell's middle. Shell gave sudden ground, short of wind. He grabbed Jesse's arms, trying to tie him up, the man's stench a miasma of rancid sweat. Jesse threw a knee to Shell's groin that broke him free, swinging for the blur of Shell's face, smashing him twice across the rocklike jaw.

Countering, Shell made a rush. Jesse's head rocked back. He tasted blood from his nose as he fought him off. After that, circling, he kept his chin low. Blocking blows with his left shoulder and forearm, he found Shell's jaw again, but there was little or no gain there. The jaw was all iron and the man didn't back up. Jesse circled, looking for an opening in the muddy light.

"Try me again, red horseman," Shell spat. "I can take anything you've got." He danced around, taunting.

Jesse moved in, sparring, and out. "Come on, horse thief."

That seemed to incite Shell. He rushed like a bull, head low, boots stomping the short grass. They both slugged away, wildly, savagely, toe to toe, both hurt, both heaving for wind, until both broke off. Jesse knew one certainty: to finish this he had to work on Shell's gut. He'd hit the granite jaw time and again without apparent advantage. In return, Shell had Jesse's head ringing, his jaw sagging, his feet wobbly, his arms leaden, his chest burning. With the back of his left hand, Jesse raked blood and sweat from his face. He circled slowly, reaching for more wind, looking for an opening.

There was none. Shell kept covering up. Jesse'd have to get at Shell's vulnerable middle, and fast, before he ran out of strength. He drove a left and right at Shell's belly and took jolting blows across his upper body, knowing that in his need to end it fast he'd hurried too much.

Next time he feinted for Shell's face. When Shell tiredly raised both blocking hands, Jesse threw all his fading strength behind a right to the belly and felt the softness there. Shell was hurt. He grunted and backed up, sucking for wind, his guard dropping. Before he could recover, Jesse rushed in and hit him twice more, then buried a right in the soft belly.

Shell let out a ragged "Ah" and doubled up, falling facedown, suddenly sick.

Jesse, weaving in his tracks, sawing for wind, stood over him, longing to smash him again. "Had enough, horse thief?"

Shell was still gagging.

"Make a move at me again," Jesse swore, "I'll kill you. That's a promise, horse thief."

Voices broke through Jesse's outer consciousness. Voices from the wagons and the ranch house. He turned. That looked like Slocum coming, holding high a lantern. Some people behind him.

"What is it?" Slocum called, looking down at Shell.

"Might ask him," Jesse said. "He jumped me." Still weaving, he made his way through the gathering to a water tank, where he stripped to his waist and washed off the blood and sweat, his body already soring up.

Standing, he thought, *It's still not over.*

Four

Lieutenant Ayers, the escort already formed, was waiting for the ox wagons to hitch up. "With good luck, we'll make Goodsight Station tonight," he told Jesse, "but we'll have to push a little. Next day into Cummings."

He stared a moment at Jesse's bruised face, swollen around the eyes and jaws, but looked away without speaking.

"You can't miss it," Jesse said, forcing a grin. "Gat Shell jumped me from behind last night when I went out to my camp. He's a tough one, all right. But I believe he got the worst of it. At least, I was the one standing when it was over. I'll have to kill him if he comes at me again."

"Maybe you should have finished the job."

Jesse shrugged. "I'd hate to shoot a man when he's flat on his belly, gagging."

Benedict loped up, the prancing black Morgan ever fighting the bit. "We took a vote and decided to head out on our own, Lieutenant. I've got nothin' agin' oxen, used to work 'em myself, but they're jest too slow for folks on the prod for Californy."

"It's your choice, Mr. Benedict, but I wish you wouldn't. The most dangerous part of the trail is from here on to Cummings."

"I figure we can handle anything that might come up. All the riders are with us, though I can't say that gambler would be much help, if all he's got is a hideout derringer." He laughed.

"Good luck, sir. Stay alert. Circle the wagons at night. Keep your stock tied inside and post guards. Be particularly on the lookout for dawn attacks. Luckily, you won't have to go through any canyons. It's open country all the way to Cummings, though some is broken and rough."

"I God, I reckon I know a little bit about Indian fightin'," Benedict said, setting his formidable shoulders. "About how far to the fort?"

"Approximately thirty-five to forty miles."

"That all? We jest might make that by evenin'."

"Be a long pull. Goodsight Station is next. Good place to camp and rest your teams."

"Jest depends how much daylight's left. If we reach Goodsight by noon, we'll keep on travelin'." He reined the stud away with a wave and loped back to his wagons.

"I knew he was going to break away sooner or later," Ayers said, shaking his head.

"You can't stop him," Jesse said.

"I would if I had the authority. No man has the right to put women and children at unnecessary risk."

While they waited, the mule-drawn wagons moved by at a brisk pace, Benedict in the lead, trailed by all the riders except Shell and Clinch. Looking back, Jesse saw the pair on the far side of the middle wagons. Shell didn't look at Jesse as he passed.

The long-striding mules took the wagons away at a rapid clip, the swaying, hooded shapes growing smaller and smaller until they disappeared in a grassy fold of undulating plain. The last sign of the train was spirals of yellow dust feathering up in the sun-shot air.

With the ox teams hitched, the three wagons got under way. Jesse thought that perhaps he felt some of Benedict's impatience at the delay and, now, the lumbering pace.

The sun-drenched morning settled into the usual monotony. Off toward Mexico, Jesse could see cone-shaped peaks standing like sentinels barring the way, the hazy distance beyond suggesting mystery and adventure. In reality, Mexico now ran red with blood. A land of shrines and churches, yet with its contradictions, its leaders capable of shocking brutality, its simple peasants of almost childlike trust and generosity, and therefore often misled. Mexican society sharply split into three classes: At the top the upper-class elite, many well-educated and property owners, dressed in silk and velvet and lace, fond of boasting about their Spanish ancestry, titled, of course. Next, the mixed-blood *Mestizos,* the small middle class, the shop-keepers and civil servants. And last, the foundation of the country, the peasant Indians, whom Jesse knew best as good soldiers, fierce at close quarters with machetes. . . . Guitar music on the plazas in the summer-soft evenings. Young people promenading in the *serenata,* the boys clockwise, the girls counterclockwise. Shy, dark, meaningful glances. Love notes being passed. Their elders watching, approving . . . A land of sharp contrasts. The very poor in peasant white and sandals and straw sombreros, and the landed, haughty *hacendados,* who had too much and wanted more and ruled like medieval war lords, brooking no interference. Indians virtual slaves on the big haciendas, unable to read or write, but who soon learned to shoot and fight and could cover fifty miles a day at a swinging dogtrot. Some bringing their families to cook and care for the wounded. "Viva Mexico! Viva Juárez! No matter no rations, *Señor* General. We'll eat cactus until times get better." . . . Father Alberto, dressed in peasant white like his patriots, returning to the hungry camp with a band of his "boys," driving cattle and leading pack-laden mules, some of the packs bloodstained. Nothing said. Cullen, tongue-in-cheek, terming the supplies "a contribution from some generous *hacendado* after a little priestly persuasion." Tonight a fiesta: beef, beans, tortillas and music. Even some wine. Nobody had more fun with less than a poor Mexican hoping for a piece of land someday to grow corn, beans and chilis. Mexico, where often style seemed more important than results in a land crying for change. Father Alberto's bleeding Mexico. . . . Good luck, *Padre.* You and President Juárez will need it when the *jefes políticos* start swarming around you in Mexico City, bowing and fawning, fat hands out, promising much, giving little or nothing in return. Good luck. Go with God. *Un abrazo, amigo.*

During his musings, he'd fallen behind, the red horse down to a slow walk, so he reined ahead to join Ayers.

The long day passed quietly, broken only by bands of curious antelopes watching the slow-moving train, their white rump patches flashing when they took flight at a flanking trooper galloping toward them in mock attack. About sundown the oxen plodded up to Goodsight, another stone and adobe station, an adobe corral and an earthen tank—but no wagons camped, no mules resting. Only fresh tracks at the tank.

"They watered and went on as we figured they'd do," Ayers said. "I feel better about their chances when I count their number of rifles. Benedict told me seven men with his wagons, counting him. Including the riders, that gives him fourteen men. Should get them through. They may have no trouble at all."

After supper, while twilight faded into sudden darkness and Ayers shared more tequila with him, Jesse said, "All we need, Lieutenant, is to hear Tattoo sounding and we'd be right at home."

"We'll be hearing that tomorrow evening at Cummings. I hope you'll stay over for a while. I want you to meet my wife, Eleanor."

"I'd like that very much. Frankly, I have no plans. Just drifting, following my instincts."

"Why not go back to Tennessee and pick up where you left off?"

"There's nothing left to go back to. My parents are gone. I have a sister in Lexington and a brother in Corinth, but . . ." He hesitated. Yet, why not talk about it? He had nothing to hide. He had no regrets, no shame for wearing the blue on the Plains, as hundreds of other Confederates had done to survive. He considered Tom Ayers a fellow soldier and an understanding friend, a newly found friend. "I did go back after my regiment was mustered out in Kansas, but old family friends turned their backs on me and walked away. I was an outcast, a pariah. They made that plain when I rode into town. Everybody I saw knew my past—everybody. Word gets around, you know. . . . My late father had disinherited me. My brother, Claiborne, three years older, who had a government job in Atlanta during the War and never fired a shot, was left the estate with Mary Elizabeth. The old farm, which I felt should have been kept in the family, was already up for sale and had buyers waiting like so many vultures. That hurt almost as much as anything, selling the old place so soon with all its memories. The good times. When we'd been a family. . . . So there's nothing to go back to."

Ayers was thoughtful for a long moment. "You could go somewhere else in the South. Start over as a teacher. Go to another state, far away. The Carolinas. Florida."

"You forget Southern pride. There will never be any forgiveness for me because I served in the Union Army in the West. No understanding why I did and why many others did. We wouldn't have fought any Reb units if there'd been any out there. That was part of the agreement when we volunteered. No—word would follow me, sure as fate, no matter where I went in the South. I'd still be an outcast—a traitor, no less."

"Why not go to a border state, say Kentucky? I have uncles back in Louisville. They're businessmen. I could send a letter of recommendation. They're fine men. My father's brothers. I know—"

Jesse stopped him. "Thank you, Lieutenant. I'm very much obliged to you. You're a generous man. I would have to decline."

"Why? We're both soldiers. You've served your country."

"I like the Southwest, wild as it is. Nobody asks a man what his name was back in the states or what he did. Maybe that's the main reason I'm here. The thing that holds me. A man can go anywhere he pleases, at his own risk. The freedom a man has in unsettled country, unfettered by traditions and false pride. Though like freedom anywhere, I guess, you have to fight to keep it sometimes. Let's drink to freedom." He passed the bottle. Losing Ana and their unborn child he could not talk about yet. It was too much. Just the thought of what had happened filled his throat, overwhelmed his senses, left him wordless.

Morning brought the promise of another clear day for travel. The ox teams seemed to form faster than usual, Ayers sent out flankers and the train moved off.

It was early afternoon when Jesse first noticed vultures circling over the trail far ahead of the train. He called them to the lieutenant's attention.

"Likely a dead animal on the trail," Ayers said.

"Maybe more than one for that many vultures."

They rode on, watching.

The terrain changed, rolling, roughing, up and down. The trail washed in places.

A flanker near the trail wheeled his mount and waved at Ayers to come on. The trooper dismounted.

Ayers spurred ahead. Jesse followed, but at that moment the mule decided to pull back on the halter rope, and Ayers had dismounted by the time Jesse rode up.

The lieutenant was bending over a hatless man on the ground. It took a moment for Jesse to recognize the tight-lipped rider who had kept to himself and watched the back trail. He looked done in, a great splotch of blood on his shirt, blood matting his long, black hair. Through cracked lips he called for water. While Ayers lifted his head, Jesse fed him water from a canteen.

He swallowed and said, "Ambushed . . . 'fraid ever'body's wiped out—," breathing in a whisper of hoarse horror. "Even women an' kids . . . on down the trail." He motioned for more water. Then "Yest'day afternoon as we's crossin' a big draw . . . they's waitin' fer us. . . . Benedict—god-damn 'im!—wouldn't put out flankers or send anybody ahead—knew it all. . . . I kept crawlin' an' crawlin'." He started coughing up blood. Ayers wiped his mouth with a bandanna. A sip of water slowed the coughing. His black eyes took on a new intensity. He was, Jesse knew, on his way out. "Name's Junius Russell. . . . Do me favor?" His eyes pleading. "Sure," Ayers said, and Jesse nodded over and over. "Write m'folks. . . . Father's Jim Russell—San Angelo, Texas. . . . I killed me a carpetbagger son of a bitch. . . . Had to make far-apart tracks. . . . U.S. marshals."

"We'll put you in a wagon," Ayers tried to assure him. "The ox teams aren't far behind."

Junius Russell didn't seem to care or hear. "Listen," he said, his voice down to a dim croak, speaking in painful gasps. "I saw 'em. . . . Hard to believe at first . . . bloody . . . horrible. . . . But I saw 'em."

"What was hard to believe?" Jesse asked, leaning closer. "What did you see?"

"I kept crawlin' after I got shot . . . they didn't see me. But I saw 'em 'round the wagons. . . . Women an' kids didn't have a chance. . . . Hard to believe. . . . An' one man's voice—I re-member it. . . . I kept hearin' it—that voice."

"What was it, Junius? What did you see besides Apaches that was hard to believe?" Jesse tipped the canteen again, but the Texan was beyond swallowing.

His lips formed a word, but he couldn't get it out. His mouth fell slack. His eyes rolled. He slumped in Ayers's arms.

"Poor devil," Ayers said. "He was trying to tell us something. Now we've got one hell of a terrible job to do."

They carried Russell off the trail. Ayers mounted and waved the other flankers in and they rode ahead in numbing dread.

They rode down a sloping draw and suddenly halted.

"My God . . ." said Ayers, averting his eyes.

Jesse looked away and back, forcing himself, biting his lower lip, feeling an old weariness and mounting shock at sight of the white shapes scattered around the skeletons of the burned wagons.

Ayers swallowed hard, told a trooper, "Halt the wagons back a way. Tell the men to keep the women and children there, then come forward to help the detail—and bring shovels."

Jesse and Ayers still sat their horses, observing the carnage, reluctant to move.

Jesse said, "Just like Junius Russell told us. Benedict was caught when the train was crossing the draw. Apaches posted all around the lip of the draw. An old tactic. Over in minutes."

They rode down to the wagons. Jesse dismounted and dropped the reins on the red horse, which didn't like the smell, but would stand.

Beside Benedict's body, bloating in the heat, they found a small mound of empty shell casings. "A brave but foolish man," Ayers said. "They took his fine Morgan stud. All those good Missouri mules. Looks like everybody dismounted and tried to make a stand by the wagons."

Most of the bodies were sprawled near the wagons, but the two young miners, lying about ten yards down the draw, apparently had made an ill-fated dash to break through the ambush. The gambler and merchant lay side by side.

"I've seen many battlefields," Jesse said, "but never bodies stripped bare before. Never any women and children. Every stitch of clothing and shoes taken from everybody, even the little children. It's ghoulish. It's chilling." His horror and outrage kept rising.

With the solemn Irish troopers, they walked over the area and back to the rutted trail, delaying what they had to do. When the men from the ox wagons joined them, it was time to get started on the gruesome duties.

They began digging a long, mass grave some yards off the trail, up where it would not wash. Next came the appalling task of moving the bodies. The troopers kept crossing themselves. One walked away and retched.

Himself sickened, Jesse paused, in even sharper pain, when he saw a golden-haired young woman lying with a protective arm around a small, golden-haired boy.

"Good God, Lieutenant," Jesse exploded, choking, his eyes filling, "the god-damned bastards even took this poor woman's wedding ring!"

"A wonder they didn't scalp her," Ayers said, looking pale.

"Apaches seldom scalp like Plains Indians. Why, I don't know. Their religion, maybe."

Jesse went to his pack for a blanket and laid it over the mother and child, weeping unashamedly.

It seemed this would never end. When it did, at last, Ayers spoke the brief service. For a headboard, they found an unburned wagon sideboard on which a trooper cut the words BENEDICT TRAIN, and another for Junius Russell, and then they went back down the trail and dug a grave for the Texan.

"Let's look the wagons over again," Ayers said. "It's the Army's duty to notify relatives, if possible. All we know about Benedict is that he said he and his people were from Arkansas."

The first wagon, at the rear of the train, still contained some broken dishes and a broken chair. The next two some scraps of clothing, a worn shoe or two, some cooking vessels, and torn sacks of grain. When they came to the last wagon, originally painted red, white and blue, now faded, a once-sturdy vehicle with the letters of the maker, THE MOLINE WAGON COMPANY, still visible, Ayers said, "I think this was Benedict's wagon. His was always the lead wagon."

Looking inside, they found mostly litter. Some loose paper. Some burned feed sacks. Some broken glass. "Picked clean as a hound's tooth of anything helpful," Ayers said, reaching for a partly charred envelope sliding on the floor in the wind. He glanced at it, started to pitch it aside, then read carefully. "This is something. It's addressed to Elijah Benedict. Fort Smith, Arkansas. We can notify the authorities there. Good." He folded and stuck the envelope inside his blouse. "The others . . . the two young miners and the gambler and the merchant . . . there's nothing we can do about them. Too bad. Junius Russell, we can."

Jesse turned to him. "In the saloon, didn't Benedict say the train carried gold to buy land in California? If my memory's right, he said the gold was in his wagon."

Ayers nodded. "That's right, he said that. Enough gold for all the families to buy land. . . . So the Apaches took the gold, too."

"But Apaches have no use for gold. A kind of taboo."

"Maybe by this time they've learned what it's worth from us White Eyes. Let's take another look around."

In thoughtful silence, they searched about the wagons again, and over the draw on both sides of the train, finding only scattered shell casings.

Leaving his mule in charge of a trooper, Jesse rode with Ayers along the draw's rim. Here and there, marked by spent shells, they saw where the ambushers had evidently concealed themselves in the grass and brush.

"From the looks of this, I'd say about twenty or so in the ambush party," Jesse said. "Now, where did they hide their horses?"

About a hundred yards beyond, in a clump of green mesquites, they found horse droppings and blood on the trampled grass.

"Somebody in the train shot straight," Ayers observed. Riding back to the draw, he said, "Two wagons are unaccounted for. There were six in all. Guess that's easy to figure. They loaded up the loot and followed the trail till they got near Cummings, then struck off into the mountains. I hope nobody coming this way was unlucky enough to run into 'em."

Jesse rubbed his jaw reminiscently. "That's not all that unaccounted for, Lieutenant. What happened to Gat Shell and his sidekick Clinch? They didn't die with the train."

Ayers stared at him. "Maybe they were at the tail end of the train and skedaddled at the first shots?"

"Shell always rode with Benedict, and Benedict always rode at the head of the train. Remember? If they did skedaddle in time, wouldn't you think they'd ride back to the safety of the escort and wagons?"

"Unless . . . unless they cut away and circled and went on the other way. They could get away from Apaches on foot at the draw. But it is strange. This whole horrible thing is strange, from Apaches taking gold and a wedding ring from a dead woman to what poor Junius Russell died trying to tell us."

Five

The afternoon was nearly gone when the ox train, having circled the ghastly draw, toiled along the trail again. After traveling for an hour, Ayers wisely called a halt and they made dry camp, circling the wagons, the three families unusually quiet, the children, solemn and big-eyed, never straying far from their elders.

"I don't expect any trouble this soon after what happened back there," Ayers said. "But they say always expect the unexpected out here."

"A good rule to live on," Jesse agreed.

"I keep thinking about Junius Russell. Whatever else he saw, it only added to the horror of what he'd witnessed. It shattered his mind."

"It's the most brutal sight I've ever seen. Brutal, even for Apaches." *Even worse than when the French mercenaries attacked the Juárista camp in the Sierra Madre, shooting indiscriminately, killing many defenseless women and children, and Ana.*

Both men said no more.

Jesse camped near the wagons. Ayers, bivouacked likewise, posted troopers around the wagons.

The night seemed to pass with troubled slowness. Roving clouds masked the stars and turned the moon to amber haze. Even the red horse and the mule stirred uneasily, Jesse thought, strangely restless. Twice, hearing hoof movement in place of grass-cropping sounds, Jesse got up to see about them. Carbine ready, he stood listening, watching the murky night. His sleep stayed broken. His mind kept flashing back to the mercenaries' attack, then to the slaughtered train, whose fate could be laid to one man, deaf to reason, drunk with conceit and bombast. It would be a long time, Jesse mused, before he could store the ordeal away with others in the further recesses of his mind.

It was late before the red horse made his usual sniffing round and quietly drifted away, before sleep came to Jesse.

His depression was still with him when Fort Cummings rose out of the northwest the next afternoon, a high-walled structure with entrance through a sally port. Above it rose a tin-roofed guard tower, flag whipping in the wind. Beyond the post, in the glittery distance, stood towering Cooke's Peak.

"Guess we part company here, Lieutenant," Jesse said, holding out a hand, when the detail formed to enter the post. "Good luck."

"Not yet, Captain. You're having supper with us tonight. I'll send an orderly for you. I suggest that you camp between the post and the spring, a few hundred yards northwest."

"I doubt that I'm fit company. I'd better decline with thanks."

"I think you need it. We both need it. Eleanor will be disappointed if you don't come."

Jesse gave in. "I'm very much obliged. I will come. Be looking forward to meeting your Eleanor. I hope I've not forgotten my manners, rusty as they are."

A chubby little boy on a spotted pony, escorted by a single trooper, left the post and swung smartly out on the trail. The bright-eyed youngster was dressed in full uniform, a sergeant's chevrons on his sleeves.

As the two trotted by, the boy sang out in a high, overofficial voice, "Good day, Lieutenant Ayers," and saluted stiffly.

He was, Jesse judged, about eight or nine years old and quite precocious. His escort, a corporal, looked bored and put upon.

"Good day to you, Sergeant Taylor," Ayers responded, returning a sweeping salute, head tilted back in exaggerated respect. "Where do your orders take you today, sir?"

"I want to ride Patches into the mountains, but the general won't let me. So it's only out on the trail a little way and back."

"You'd better follow the general's orders or you'll end up in the guardhouse," Ayers said sternly. "In addition, you'd get busted back to private."

"Someday I'll ride right into the mountains, all the way through the canyon and back."

"Under escort, you mean, Jaime. And a great big maybe at that. The mountains are always off bounds to you. Well, have a good ride, Sergeant, and good day to you, Corporal."

The boy spurred his pony and away they dashed, the corporal doggedly at his side.

"Not the most sought-after duty, shepherding a spoiled but likable boy," Ayers said, smiling. "Corporal Daly must have committed a dastardly breech of discipline to be assigned such duty. Truth is, the adjutant tries to pass the job around. Daly draws it most often and the boy likes him. Yet I'd say it beats cleaning stables. The General is Colonel Richard R. "Fighting Dick" Taylor, a brevet brigadier in the war, and don't you forget it, sir. Jaime is the Taylors' only son. I'll save the rest for tonight."

The spring was a big one. Jesse watered his thirsty stock, filled his canteens from habit and chose a camping place in the mesquites well off the trail. The three ox wagons drew up near the spring.

How did a man prepare for going out to supper with genteel people? He'd almost forgotten. He began with a cavalryman's bath, achieved by bringing more water from the spring, and soap and towel from his pack, and trimming his beard with scissors and the aid of a hand mirror. In it was a face he seldom saw, like a stranger's. An older face. One that favored the carefree South Carolina Alden side of the family, it was said: fair and the features evenly molded, long ago burned golden brown by sun and wind. A straight nose, neither too long nor too short. Gray eyes set wide, wrinkled at the corners. A full mouth fixed in a thoughtful expression, a touch of sadness etched there. He tried to shake it off. *I'll be damned,* he lectured himself, *if I'll give in to self-pity. I will not.* It could, he knew, wreck a man, leave him unable to function in his present dangerous world.

He looked at the slash of naked scalp high above his right ear. A minié ball at Franklin had marked him thus. But Franklin's deeper scars weren't visible at all: part of his cast of nightmares, his demons, among them the lone ghostly horseman in close pursuit, swinging his saber. He regarded his white hair, which hung to his shoulders and belonged to a much older man. Yet, in a way, it fit because he was much older than his years. Rebuking himself for dwelling again on the past, he set about trimming his hair with the scissors. Maybe the post barber could make further improvements tomorrow, if Jesse thought of it.

He found a clean blue flannel shirt, a pair of decent gray trousers, brushed his boots and hat, and was as ready as he could be. He frowned, thinking of a possible appropriate gift for the hostess. Digging into his pack, he remembered a shiny silver ornament bearing a carved Aztec face, a nugget of blue turquoise for a crown, purchased on his ride out of Mexico from a peasant craftsman, mainly because he liked the deep color of the turquoise.

As the afternoon faded, he found himself listening to the familiar sounds coming from the post, the commands and movements, feeling an isolation that surprised him. Yet, he realized, he had lived too long by army routine, South and North, not to miss some of its well-ordered regime. He caught the ensuing clatter of hooves and equipment when the bugler blew Stables. At sunset, with the sun sliding down behind the mountains, leaving deep purple shadows on this side, he heard the bugler sound Retreat and he pictured the assembled garrison and the lowering of the flag.

A little later a private strode up to his camp.

"Mr. Wilder, sor?" His Irish brogue was thick.

"Yes."

"Lieutenant Ayers presents his compliments," the trooper said, at the same time sizing up the red horse and mule. "It's me honor to escort ye to the post, past the guard, and to direct ye to the lieutenant's quarters."

"Mighty fine. Thank you."

The trooper glanced again at the horse as they walked off. "I hope ye keep a close watch on yer stock."

"I try to."

"We keep ours corralled inside at night. If we didn't, we'd soon be afoot."

A true worry, Jesse thought. One he hadn't overlooked. One he'd have to see about later. But nobody, not even an Indian, could mount the picketed red horse bareback.

Inside the quadrangle, he caught at once the close odors of stables, dust, gun oil, leather, and the supper smells, all blended into one.

The trooper directed him to where Ayers waited beneath the brush-roofed ramada of his quarters. Jesse crossed over. Ayers shook hands warmly. "Come in. Come in. Meet the officer in charge."

Eleanor Ayers greeted him as warmly, her expressive hazel eyes alive with anticipation as she extended a gracious hand. "Please come in, Captain. Tom has told me so much about you."

"By now it's plain Jesse," he said, smiling back at her, already liking her very much. Her eyes flicked to his white hair only for an instant.

She was slender and dark-haired, younger than the lieutenant, barely coming to her lanky husband's shoulder. Her slim face seemed all big, warm eyes, accented even more by the way she wore her hair swept back and tied on her neck. She had a sweet, generous mouth and her smile was constant. She wore a light blue dress cut low in front which showed an expanse of ivory bosom.

"Please sit down," she said, a hint of the South in her soft tones.

Momentarily taken by her greeting, he had almost forgotten his gift. He took it from a coat pocket and held it out for her, saying, "Here is something for you from Mexico. I wish it had a pin or clasp."

Her open-mouthed surprise was akin to that of a child. She looked up at him and exclaimed, "Thank you so much. It's beautiful—the face, the turquoise. I adore it."

"I think it's some Aztec king," Jesse said, "but even the artist didn't know his name."

"Maybe it's one of the Montezumas," she said, regarding it closely. "I've read about the Aztecs. Their civilization was advanced long before Cortez invaded Mexico."

"—and promptly put to ruin what they'd built up over the centuries," Tom Ayers said.

"They developed a surprisingly accurate chronological table," she went on, ignoring the interruption. "It shows an advanced knowledge of astronomy, which is in sharp contrast with some of their . . . ah . . . practices."

"—such as taking captives as human sacrifices for the gods," her husband broke in. "Particularly, beautiful young girls."

"Jesse," she said, displaying mock annoyance, "there's nothing like an interruptive husband who won't let his poor wife finish a single thought. What do you think of such behavior in a grown man reportedly educated at West Point, that reported bastion of good manners?"

He smiled, thinking it would be difficult not to smile at Eleanor Ayers. "I believe I'd better straddle the fence on that."

"Why, dear, I was just afraid some of the squeamishness you gleaned at Miss Greenfield's Finishing School in Baltimore might cause you to leave out the needed facts—that was all," Ayers said, bowing from the waist.

She turned her back on him to regard the ornament again in more detail. "So you have no name, you and your blue crown. I shall call you Monty, and put you away for now while a certain lieutenant of horse pours our thoughtful guest a drink. Excuse me, Jesse."

She went into another room. *A true Army wife and hostess,* Jesse thought, *gracious and quick to make a guest feel at ease. One who would put up with the many discomforts of post life in the West, while maintaining her poise and sense of humor, and making do with limited supplies from the commissary.* The quarters were Spartan, Jesse saw, but clean and bright. Blue-and-white curtains at the single window. A rose-colored piece of carpet on the rammed-dirt floor. A pine table on which sat a tall kerosene lamp with a decorated shade. A two-shelf wooden bookcase crammed with books and magazines. On the adobe walls several nostalgic prints of wooded scenes and streams. He supposed they would eat in the kitchen. It didn't matter. This was a home. Tom and Eleanor had made it so, the twitting at each other a sign of love and happiness. Seeing and sensing all this, he felt the last of his initial stiffness leave him.

Only moments had passed before Eleanor returned, Ayers after her, holding two glasses of amber-colored drinks in one hand and a glass of wine in the other for her. He handed Jesse a glass and, raising his own, said, "Here's how," to which Jesse responded, "And to you and Eleanor, a most gracious hostess."

The unexpected toast brought color to her face. "Tom, we must manage somehow to keep Jesse with us for a while."

"I've been racking my brain."

As they sat and Jesse tasted his drink, he experienced an immediate pleasure. "I do believe," he said in wonder, "I am actually tasting aged Kentucky bourbon for the first time in years. It's as smooth as spring water."

Ayers beamed. "You are. Thanks to the post trader's connections. By way of the long haul from Fort Union, east of Santa Fe. Served only on special occasions. Not forgetting the good tequila you shared with me in bivouac."

"My pleasure."

They chatted on lightly, both men avoiding any reference to the slaughtered wagon train, though doubtless, Jesse thought, Tom had told Eleanor. In turn, she was doing her best to make Jesse feel at ease. "Tom's been telling me about your beautiful horse, which he says is the color of copper. Did you get him in Mexico?"

"I bought him from a trader in El Paso, as I've told Tom. I liked the bold look in his eyes, the way he held his head. He once ran wild. He'll always be wild in spirit. I broke him to ride, after he threw me and threw me. Sometimes I think he only tolerates me. I think a good deal of him. At night he's like a sentry. Very alert, suspicious of any sounds, anything that moves, or any new smells." Jesse sipped his drink. "I'm afraid I'm like the fellow in Shakespeare who did nothing but talk about his horse."

"Please, go on," she said.

"Well, at night, when camped, he comes over and sniffs me to see if I'm all right. That is, I suppose that's the reason. But he won't come up to me in daytime when he's on picket. I have to go to him. However, he will let me pet him."

She clapped her hands. "I'd love to see him."

"I'll see that you do."

"Eleanor and the other ladies ride occasionally beyond the post, always with an escort," Ayers said. "In that connection, I am concerned that you are camped outside the post."

"Yes," she agreed.

"There's always some danger in Apache country," Jesse said. "You have to learn to look out for yourself and your stock."

She glanced at her husband, a reminding look, and he said, "I know your plans are indefinite, Jesse. But upon reporting in this afternoon, I found out something that may interest you. . . . Our post scout, Alamo Pierce, quit while the escort was gone. Said he was going back to East Texas. I'm not surprised. He never impressed me. He claimed he knew the country, but it was mostly blow and show. Went around dressed in fringed buckskins. Wore two big pistols. Hung out at the post trader's most of the time, hoping somebody would buy him a drink, for which he had an astounding capacity. The adjutant said the Old Man was about to discharge him anyway. Maybe Pierce saw it coming."

Jesse reflected on that. "You said Pierce didn't know the country well. I don't know it at all."

"You could learn it fast. From helping escort woodcutting details into the mountains and immigrants through Cooke's Canyon, to other general duties and map study. This part of New Mexico is well mapped."

"Maps help, but I never saw one that located the water holes. To really know an area, you have to ride over it. How long did Pierce serve as scout?"

"Less than four months. Drifted in here from Arizona. Said he'd been scout at Fort Lowell. We needed a scout, so the Old Man took him on without checking with Lowell. Frankly, I think Pierce was just working his way east."

"What happened to the scout before Pierce?"

Ayers looked at his wife before he answered. "That was Art Kimes. Got ambushed on the Mimbres River. He was green at the game, but a good man. We hated to lose him."

"Too bad."

"The pay is one twenty-five a month," Ayers stressed. "Same as a second lieutenant's."

Jesse would need the money before long. His infrequent pay with the Juáristas, either in pesos or gold, depended on when Father

Alberto could use his "persuasive powers" on some wealthy *hacendado* to "contribute" to the cause. "I'm weary of war. I haven't told you, Tom, that besides the Army of Tennessee and out west with the blue, I also served in Mexico. Another ex-Reb—Cullen Floyd, a Mississippian—and I trained a little army of Juárista peasants to fight the French and their mercenaries of the Emperor Maximilian."

Ayers sat back, his eyes intent. "Tell us about the training. And about Maximilian."

"In all fairness to him," Jesse reflected, "and what I could make out from the other side, he struck me as a man who meant well. But the French used him as an international pawn or dupe—he was Austrian, you know, an archduke. The French cast him aside. Maximilian was executed at Querétaro a few weeks ago. I left the same day, after pleading with President Juárez to spare his life and two Mexican generals. To me, and many Mexicans, the execution was cruel and unnecessary." He held back. Was he sounding self-important? But the rapt attention of his listeners urged him to continue. He said then, feeling a long-needed ease, "I can tell you that we turned out good infantrymen, once they learned organization, to respect superiors and how to fire in order and maneuver in company and battalion strength. Many had never fired a rifle. But they could use machetes with deadly effect at close quarters—merciless when attacking and didn't like to take prisoners. Sometimes they had to be restrained, to be ordered back."

"Go on," Ayers urged.

"Please do," Eleanor said.

"As infantry, the Juáristas could cover as much ground as an Apache at a swinging dogtrot. Fifty or more miles a day. After all, many are pure Mexican Indians. So we trained Indians and mixed-blood *Mestizos,* who were just as good, imbued with the same cause. There were no haughty Spaniards of alleged noble birth in our ranks carrying smuggled-in Enfields." As much as he'd like to, he would not reveal how he and Cullen and a band of hard-riding Juáristas had cracked the armory at Fort Bliss, near El Paso, and packed off a hundred-odd Spencer repeating rifles and much ammunition. Nor would he tell about the slippery arms smuggler and two henchmen shot dead in town when they tried to take Juárista gold without handing over the agreed rifles. "The Spanish *hacendados* down there hold themselves aloof from the common Mexican peon—until they take some poor, frightened Mexican girl to bed. . . . I'm proud to tell you about the battles we won. We whipped the French Foreign Legion at San Juan de Río and took many prisoners, and we stormed the Presidio Montaña—battered it with a twelve-pounder Napoleon we took apart and hauled on our backs to a church tower. And we gunned down the notorious Colonel Dubray and his staff trying to escape. . . . I'm proud of the Juárista peasant soldiers. They seemed to know no fear and they didn't complain. They could go day after day on a handful of pinole, mixed with water and sweetened with panocha, and maybe a piece of dried beef."

He stopped and looked at them. While Eleanor sat in awed silence, Ayers filled the glasses again.

"I'm talking way too much," Jesse said.

"Not at all," Ayers said. "This is very interesting from a military standpoint and from your own personal experiences. I sensed more had happened in Chihuahua than a few brushes with Apaches. Go on. You know you're among friends, and after what you've been through, maybe it needs to be said."

"Yes," Eleanor said. "By all means continue."

And so he told them about Cullen Bradford Floyd, and how, leading his last charge, in his excitement he'd shouted, "Come on, boys! We've got the god-damned Yankees on the run!" By then, both Rebs promoted to citizen generals by order of Juárez. And he told them about Father Alberto Garza, a humble little man of vague years in peasant white and sandals, astride a brown mule. A magnetic little man with a beautiful speaking voice, who spoke five languages fluently and without military experience had formed a peasant army. How his people wanted to call him General, as some bandoleered guerilla leaders did with only fifty men, but he'd have none of that. It was always plain Father Alberto.

And he told them about a proud *hacendado* named Sedillo whom Jesse had stopped from executing prisoners, forced him to back down at gunpoint, humiliated him before hundreds of Juáristas. How some days later while napping in his tent Jesse woke to find Sedillo pointing a rifle at him.

"He was a fair-weather patriot who hadn't joined us with his cowed peons until he was certain the French faced defeat. He called me a gringo and told me to get ready to die because I'd insulted him. I knew he meant what he said. I'd never seen such haughty hate filling a man's face. I was alone, no weapon at hand. We had just taken San Luis Potosí without firing a shot, the French retreating toward Querétaro. Cullen had gone into town with most of the army to celebrate."

For a lingering moment Jesse saw the scene again in every detail. "I heard him say, 'We Sedillos never forget an insult. You are going to die for that, gringo. Let's see if you can die like a man, like the Southern *Americano* you claim to be.' He spat the words at me. I just stood there, frozen, thinking I'd leap at him, but knowing there wasn't time. He lifted the rifle higher.

"There was a blast of gunfire, but somehow I felt no pain. Sedillo collapsed at my feet. Then Father Alberto stepped from the door of the tent. The *padre,* who had never fired a shot in battle, held a smoking pistol in his right hand. I remember he said something about Mexico not forsaking a friend. His hand was shaking. I asked him if he wanted me to take the pistol. He looked at it and said, 'No, we still have a way to go.'

"A great man, the little *padre,*" Jesse said thoughtfully. "I think of him often. As for myself, looking back at all that's happened, from the war between the North and the South to now, somehow I've always been a survivor—the damned survivor. All my boyhood friends died in the war. Every last one of them. Most of them at Shiloh, then the few left at Franklin, where Tom likewise lost his dear father. . . . Why couldn't it have been me instead of one of them? Why not me instead of Cullen, who passed on longing for home and the father who'd disowned him for wearing the blue in the West . . . and all I could tell him was, 'Home is where we are.'

"There are still times when I feel a burden of guilt because I survived and others didn't." His voice broke a little. To his embarrassment, he was close to tears. He dared not talk about Ana.

"Oh, no," Eleanor said, "you shouldn't feel that way." Her eyes were wet.

"Not at all," said her husband. "That's war—the chances men take."

The awkward moment passed, and Jesse regained his composure.

"I guess I'm finally finished," he said. "War is such a terrible experience, or I should say, a series of horrible experiences. I'm grateful to you for listening. I guess everything has come full circle here this evening. A sort of summing up. From the day my friends and I all marched off to the sounds of 'Dixie' and the 'Bonnie Blue Flag,' while in the North other boys were marching to 'John Brown's Body' and the 'Battle Hymn of the Republic.'"

He smiled then, and lifted his glass to them.

At a lantern-lit dinner in the cramped little kitchen they talked of current matters, making a special effort to put war behind them: general post gossip, the sense of isolation and shortages of supplies, all provisions coming from far away Fort Union, the passing immigrants and their never-ending hopes of finding new homes in Arizona and California. While Jesse, eating heartily, praised her dinner, Eleanor apologized for the corned beef and dried peas, beans cooked with bacon, fresh baked bread and only one fresh vegetable from the post garden.

"You're just hungry," she said.

"I am," he replied, "but this is very good food. Mighty good. I'm surprised Tom can climb to the saddle."

"Most nights I feed him straight field rations, which keep him slim."

And when Jesse remarked on the "delicious apple pie," she looked at her husband in pretended apology, and he said, "I have to confess that she's pulled the wool over your eyes, Jesse. Her apple pie is nothing but lowly soda crackers flavored with cinnamon and lemon extract—only that."

"I swear I can taste the peel," Jesse replied gallantly.

"Shows just one of the many ways a woman can fool a man. It was months, and then only by taking sneak peeks, before I learned how she was making apple pies when there weren't any apples."

"I'm working on a recipe for make-believe peach cobbler," she twitted him, "but the ingredients shall remain absolutely secret. No peeks allowed, Lieutenant."

After supper, while the men had brandy, Ayers said, "I want to tell you about the Old Man. I'd like you two to meet. He has a keen interest in the recent military developments in Mexico, and is thinking of writing a history."

"Would he want to talk to a former Reb?"

"All the more reason, especially in view of what you've been through. A rare firsthand opportunity. He made quite a record for himself in the Virginia campaigns. I do admire the man."

"You called him Fighting Dick."

"A name that stuck with him after Kelly's Ford on the Rappahannock in 'sixty-three. Fitzhugh Lee's cavalry had felled trees and posted sharpshooters in rifle pits on the south bank. Three times squadrons of dismounted Union cavalry tried to force a crossing and were thrown back. Finally, the Old Man, then a major, and a party of twenty men fought their way across and through the felled timber. That enabled the command to follow. When the fighting at the ford ended, he discovered that bullets had pierced his uniform in five places. His mount had been hit three times. A five-hour battle followed, and he was also in the thick of that. It was an all-cavalry fight." He broke off, looking directly at Jesse. "Here I am back on the war again. I don't mean to wear you out."

"You aren't at all. The general is an interesting man. Tell me more about him."

"Kelly's Ford was in March. For that he was promoted one grade. Not long after, to a full colonel. In June, at Brandy Station, he again distinguished himself with conspicuous gallantry, leading charge after charge. For that, he made brigadier."

"I have the feeling he's a strict disciplinarian," Jesse said.

"That he is—but a martinet only in the case of deserters. Before we came out, a deserter absconded with several thousand dollars from the post trader's safe. A detail caught him the other side of Goodsight Station. Brought him back lashed facedown across the saddle for the rest of the garrison to see. An object lesson for anyone thinking of going over the hill. A Corporal Fogel—Karl Fogel. A troublemaker. They said he'd been busted so many times he put his chevrons on with hooks and eyes. He wasn't riding a cavalry mount, as you'd expect. Somehow he'd managed for a good horse, which he'd staked out in the mesquites. . . . Since neither a summary court nor a special court can adjudge a dishonorable discharge, and a general court-martial can be authorized only by department commanders or the President of the United States, the Old Man acted on his own. He ordered Fogel flogged fifty times—even though the Army abolished flogging in 'sixty-one—the letter *D* branded on each cheek, his head shaved and drummed out of the cavalry. They say Fogel never flinched or batted an eye through all that. Tough man. Went out of the sally-port gate cussing everybody and swearing revenge. . . . Well, enough of that," Ayers said, looking at his wife.

She shuddered. "Did you have to tell us that?"

"The story could be harsher. The detail could have been under verbal instructions, which don't go into the official order and record, to bring Fogel back dead or alive." His quick smile erased her frown and he turned back to Jesse. "The Old Man does keep the command busy, but not too rigidly. As you know, there can be a good deal of boredom in a remote post like this. But if men aren't kept busy, they can fall into slothful ways and order will suffer. Apache alarms keep us on our toes. Except for plenty of good water and army soap keeping us clean, living conditions are generally . . . how shall I say it, Eleanor?"

"Somewhat trying at times," she said with a laugh. "But it's home—our first home—and I wouldn't live anywhere else, if it meant separating us."

Jesse, admiring her, paid her his silent tribute again: *a true army wife. A fine young woman.*

"Tom," she said, "has tacked a rubber sheet to the ceiling of our bedroom so centipedes won't drop on us. We put the legs of our bed in cans of water to keep red ants from crawling in with us. He turns his boots upside down every morning to check for tarantulas, and I've been careful opening kitchen cabinet doors ever since I found a huge rattlesnake napping there."

"What did you do?" Jesse asked.

"Tom was on escort duty. I ran outside and shouted for the sergeant of the guard. Four troopers were there in less than half a minute. But guess who got Mr. Snake out? Me! They just stood around until I got a hold of Mr. Snake with a stove shovel and a long fork and escorted him outside—then the brave troopers took over."

Her account, told with fearful grimaces and a step-by-step re-enactment of her courageous struggle, had both men laughing.

More light talk followed, and another brandy, which furthered more talk, and suddenly, too suddenly, the evening had spent itself. When Taps sounded, Jesse rose to go and paid his respects.

Eleanor thanked him for "Monty" and gave him a kiss on the cheek. Ayers, shaking hands, said, "Think about the scout's job. I believe I can get it for you. I've already put a bug in the Old Man's ear. We need a man with experience."

"But one who knows the country," Jesse said. He thanked them again and bade them good night.

The guard let him out of the gate.

A cool night wind, gamboling out of the mountains, was a playful voice around his ears, now near, now flouncing away, as if beckoning him to follow. The sky, swept clear of clouds for a change, was a star-speckled dome. A rising first-quarter moon was growing bolder. Everything around him was in tune with his mood. An evening like this, he thought, was what a drifting man missed most: the company of warmhearted people, good food and drink, lively conversation, and tonight the plus of a young couple laughing at little hindrances, and their light teasing of each other—that was love.

Nearing camp, he found his picketed friends grazing quietly, dark shapes among the darker mesquites. The red horse stirred at his approach and Jesse knew that he was being watched. He stayed motionless; so did the horse, still watching, still wary. Only when Jesse went to his pack did the horse resume grazing. *Our little game,* Jesse thought, always amused. *He smelled me.* In his blankets, he watched the sky, aware of a sense of peace he hadn't known for a long time. Night sounds took over. A coyote's high-pitched song in the foothills, answered by other coyotes. A few night birds. Wind rustling the mesquites. At the fort the sentries calling "All's well" on the hour from post to post.

He had no idea how long he'd been sleeping when he opened his eyes, wide awake at once, aroused by a wrongness. Much of the night had passed. In surprise, he noted a faint pink brushing the eastern sky. He'd slept far more soundly than usual, even missing his horse's vigilant presence, too soundly for his demons to reappear and march tauntingly across the stage of his mind.

His senses warned him something was different. A change in the usual rhythm of the desert night. He'd felt it; something had broken his sleep. Some scrap of sound. Something subtle. Too, his horse had moved suddenly. Not just his occasional stirring while grazing. This was an abrupt movement, a sign of alertness, of suspicion.

Rolling over, Jesse drew the Spencer and slowly sat up. He heard nothing wrong, only the wind, which had dropped to a low murmur. But his inner sense that the night still wasn't right wouldn't go away. Instincts again, time-trusted instincts, and nearby the once-wild horse on picket. Rising in his stocking feet, Jesse eared back the carbine's hammer and opened his eyes wider, straining to see. He spotted the mule first, grazing contentedly.

But the horse wasn't grazing. He stood like a statue, swung around toward the dark blur of the foothills, watching, watching.

Jesse watched that way also, but there was only muddy blackness to see. Before very long, in minutes, first light would lay a golden tint on the hills. He kept watching the hills, trusting his horse. Only sensing, not seeing.

He was unprepared, frozen for an instant, when from the direction of the hills, but in close, rising from the ground, a figure started slipping along the horse's picket line.

The red horse snorted, swung away.

The figure moved faster.

At that moment, Jesse pulled the trigger.

The figure seemed to jerk with the carbine's bang. Crying out, it whirled toward Jesse, who snapped the trigger guard down, ejecting the empty case and recharging the chamber. His second shot drove the thief backward and down. He did not rise.

Reloading, Jesse stepped deeper into the cover of a mesquite, swiveling his gaze back and forth, looking for others. Only the horse moved, dancing, watching. The mule had stopped grazing. Daylight was on its way. From the fort rose shouts for sergeant of the guard.

After some seconds, Jesse decided this was a lone horse thief. He'd probably spotted the red horse from the vantage of the hills during the afternoon. Still, Jesse waited, searching for nearby movement between him and the hills.

Not until daylight splashed over the mesquites did he go to the unmoving shape on the ground. He prodded it with a toe. The man didn't stir. To Jesse's surprise, the dead man was an Indian dressed like a white man: boots, pants, shirt. An Indian in braids. But he wasn't Apache.

Jesse turned at the racket of a detail hurrying from the fort. He heard Tom Ayers calling his name.

"Over here," Jesse called back. "Over here."

They came through the mesquites, carbines ready, and advanced toward him. Ayers and a squad.

"You all right, Jesse?"

"I am. I want you to look at this dead horse thief. There was just one."

"Looks like a white man except for the braids," the Lieutenant said, staring down.

"Point is," Jesse said, "he's not Apache. No moccasins or leggings or breechcloth or headband. No hair down to his shoulders."

"What do you think he is?"

Jesse turned the Indian over so that the face was up. There was a knife at his belt. "He's not Sioux or Cheyenne or Comanche—that I've seen. I believe he's an Eastern Indian. Take your pick of a dozen tribes."

"An Eastern Indian way out here. Hmm. What do you make of it?"

"I don't. He should be Apache. Kinda strange."

"Strange as hell, I'd say. I think the Old Man will want to see you and know about this no later than this morning. I'll get word to you."

Six

Accompanied by an orderly sent soon after Guard Mount Call, Jesse entered headquarters. Lieutenant Ayers took him into an inner office and made the introductions, addressing Colonel Taylor as "General" and Jesse as "Mr. Wilder."

Taylor was a spare, lean-faced man of energetic manner. His neatly trimmed mustache and beard brought out the prominence of his thrusting jaw. A fighting jaw, one might judge. Jesse guessed he was about forty years old. He rose from behind his desk and shook hands, an appraising interest in his bold eyes.

"At ease, Mr. Wilder," he said, and waved Jesse to a chair. "I understand you had some excitement in camp early this morning."

"Yes, sir. An Indian was trying to steal my horse on picket."

"At first we thought it was an attack on the ox-drawn wagons near the spring. We know we are under constant observation and threat here. If the rump-spring geniuses in Washington ever see fit to provide me with more than just enough men to maintain this post, I'd do something about that. Lieutenant Ayers tells me that the Indian was not Apache, judging by his dress and hair."

"He was not."

"Besides his dress, do you have any other basis for your opinion?"

"Dress is the main reason. I've also fought Apaches in Chihuahua. None wore braids or dressed like white men. They would consider that a disgrace and be subjected to ridicule by their people."

"Any guesses, then, as to the thief's tribe?"

"Not a Plains Indian, certainly. Maybe a Delaware or a Shawnee. They're good scouts and have been hired by parties of whites going west. It's just a guess and in no way explains why an Eastern Indian would show up in Southern New Mexico trying to steal a horse. To me, it's very strange."

"No stranger than what's been happening on the trail between here and Mesilla. I've just read Lieutenant Ayers's report. Ambushed immigrants stripped to their last stitch of clothing and pieces of jewelry, even a wedding ring. Wagons obviously loaded with loot being driven off toward the Mimbres Mountains—the last most uncharacteristic of Apaches, though I can visualize it being done with pack mules—and it's not the first time it's happened." Taylor kept shifting restlessly in his chair as he talked. A thought seemed to occur to him. "Mr. Ayers has told me briefly of your unusual service as a soldier, for both the South and later the North on the western frontier, Mr. Wilder, and recently in Chihuahua, training Juáristas."

"That is true," Jesse said.

"It happens that I am a rather keen student of military history. Not only of our war, but also of the defeat of Maximilian's trained troops, including the French Foreign Legion, by a peasant army. In the near future, I plan to write a history on that conflict, also touching on the political aspects."

"The little peasant army that another ex-Confederate and I trained wasn't the only peasant force, General. I believe Diaz had another army, and there could have been another or two. There was no communication between the peasant armies. We never knew what Diaz was doing, except in what state he was operating, and I'm sure he didn't know our location until the final drive to Querétaro. Neither did we often know where President Juárez was."

"One thing I'm getting at is this. There's a gap in what I've been able to dig up on what really happened at San Juan de Río. What little there was in the newspapers. What really turned the tide there, Mr. Wilder?"

"We knew we couldn't take the fort. No artillery. We had to draw them out where we could get at 'em." Jesse looked up, reliving the beginning of the battle.

Taylor could hardly wait. "What did you do? What tactic?"

"Our objective was to draw them out, but without showing what strength we had. So we posted sharpshooters in the timber with Enfields, firing at sentries on the wall. Meantime, we slipped a company armed with Spencer repeating rifles down a brush-covered wash. Our other Spencer company we kept under cover in the timber." *Should he have brought in the Spencers? Well, why not? Tell the truth. Someday, maybe, this war would see the light of print. But leave out how the Spencers were obtained.*

Taylor pounced on that. "Spencers, you say?"

Jesse had let that slip out. "Only two companies," he went on composedly. "The rest armed with old Enfields, shotguns, old Ballard carbines, a few Sharps rifles—anything the Juáristas could buy from gun runners on the Rio Grande."

Taylor was taking notes, scribbling fast with a pencil. He quit suddenly and drilled Jesse with a look. "I've been told that a band of men, reportedly Juáristas, broke into the Fort Bliss armory and got away with a hundred or more Spencers and much ammunition."

"When was that?" Jesse asked innocently.

"Within the year. A sizable reward has been posted."

Jesse shrugged. "Gun dealers come in all colors, General, and our Spencers came from wherever the *padre* could buy arms."

"The *padre?*"

"Father Alberto Garza, the unsung hero of the war. A man of God, a man of the Mexican poor, defrocked by the Church because he sided with President Juárez, who had separated church and state in his *Leyes de Reforma,* expelled the archbishop and bishops. I believe the United States had recognized Juárez as president."

"That is true."

"Although Father Garza knew nothing about war, he personally put together our little army, which you could call the Army of Northern Chihuahua. His magnetism was astonishing. The peasants would follow him anywhere. The other ex-Reb who did the training was my good friend Cullen Bradford Floyd from Mississippi. He died in battle."

"Both Mr. Wilder and Floyd were citizen generals," Ayers put in.

"More of what I need," Taylor said, busy jotting that down. "This sheds new light on what actually happened down there and swung the tide for Juárez. This is the first I've heard of former Confederates training Juáristas. It's common knowledge that a number of them joined Maximilian. Did you ever come against your former comrades?"

"Only once, when we overran a wagon train of French regulars north of San Luis Potósi. With the escort was a little handful of Rebs from Bate's Brigade, the 37th Georgia, and Bushrod Johnson's Brigade, the 17th Tennessee. We took them prisoner and later released 'em. They had put up a stiff fight. I think most of the Rebs with Maximilian must have been posted around Mexico City, farther south from where we operated."

"Now," Taylor said, with anticipation, "tell me all about what happened at San Juan de Río, which I understand was a pivotal fight and broke the French power in the north."

For the next hour Jesse described the battle from beginning to end, step by step, detail after detail, many coming to mind for the first time in months, while Taylor wrote furiously, now and then breaking in with questions.

"But the notorious Colonel Dubray escaped," Jesse concluded.

"Colonel Dubray . . . why notorious? Tell me about him."

"At his orders, the French and the Hussars were pillaging the district. Not just foraging for supplies, but raping and murdering, hanging dissenters in the plaza to discourage others."

"How did he escape?"

"When he saw the battle was lost, he and his staff rode out the fort's rear gate."

"Did you cut his tracks again?"

"We did at the Presidio Montaña. Caught up with him, you might say. In the final stages of the battle, he tried the same escape he had at San Juan de Río—through the rear gate. But this time we were waiting for him and his staff."

"Yes?" Taylor hurried him.

"He was dressed in a gold-braided uniform and plumed helmet.

Very showy. They charged us, sabers out. I shot him twice. The second bullet knocked him from the saddle. I can still see the arrogance in that mustached face as he went down. In it the epitome of all the suffering and cruelty he'd caused."

The room seemed unusually quiet. Taylor's eyes were sharply observant. "Was there something personal in that, General Wilder?"

"Yes, sir. Dubray had led the raid on the Juárista camp that, among others, killed my Mexican wife, Ana, and our unborn child. Yes, it was personal and a matter of honor to avenge them."

At last it was out of him.

Taylor had quit writing. "I'm very sorry to hear that, sir. Realizing all this brings back those painful memories . . . would you feel like going into the details of the Presidio Montaña battle?"

"Glad to, General. I think the story should be told."

There was a racket in the anteroom. A trooper's chiding voice, light, rapid footsteps, and round-faced Jaime Taylor bounded into the office, wearing his sergeant's uniform, calling, "Papa, Papa."

"Jaime, you know you're never to interrupt me," his father said, nevertheless taking the boy in his arms.

"I want to ride Patches," the boy sniffed, "but nobody'll take me now."

"You'll have to wait until this afternoon, when Corporal Daly has time. He has other duties, you know."

"I want to go now, Papa. By myself, if the corporal can't go."

"You know the rules. You never ride without an escort—never. Absolutely never." Taylor glanced at Ayers and Jesse, his expression that of an abiding parent trying to correct a beloved and overindulged child. "You're also forgetting your manners, Sergeant Taylor. Show proper respect to an officer by saluting Lieutenant Ayers and saying hello to Mr. Wilder."

At that, Jaime got down and saluted Ayers, who returned a severe salute, and bowing respectfully to Jesse, said, "Hello, Mr. Wilder."

"Hello. I'm very glad to know you, Sergeant Taylor." Jesse snapped a salute, then held out a quick hand.

That broke the ice. The boy smiled engagingly and shook hands. "Tom—I mean Lieutenant Ayers—is my friend. I hope you will be, too."

"I believe we are already friends, Jaime."

The boy's smile broadened. Behind the blue eyes Jesse could see something working, and Jaime said, "As my new friend, you can be my escort. We can go riding now."

"I would like to ride with you, Jaime. But the general means a military escort this afternoon, and you don't disobey a general."

The boy pouted a little, then flashing his engaging smile, he romped out the room.

"Sorry about the interruption, Mr. Wilder," Taylor said. "I'm the first to admit that Jaime is somewhat spoiled, try as my wife and I do not to give in too much to an only child."

"You want a boy to be a boy," Jesse said understandingly. "I see a cavalryman in the making, General."

"Thank you. I hope so. There are worse careers for a young man to follow, though I can't say it's a lucrative one. Could we talk again soon—say tomorrow—about the Presidio Montaña battle? I'd appreciate that very much. I want to put down every detail that you remember. It's an unknown, even neglected, phase of the war in Mexico, and will remain so, I'm afraid, unless I do so. It's a rare opportunity to record military history made by a principal participant, Citizen General Wilder. A successful general at that."

"I'm obliged, sir. Glad you think it's important. For me, I just want to put it all behind me."

Taylor looked apologetic. "I hope I'm not interfering with your plans?"

"As I've told Lieutenant Ayers, I'm just drifting west. Frankly, I'm trying to get a hold of myself again, which I will in time."

"I can well understand that. You have my very deepest sympathy about your wife and child and your good friend." Ayers was nodding the same. Taylor stood. "I have something in mind which I hope you will consider carefully. . . . I am offering you the position of civilian scout at Fort Cummings."

Taken aback, Jesse could only stare at him. He started to refuse, but Taylor said, "Give yourself time to think about it, time to consider. We'll talk about it tomorrow after Mounted Drill sounds." A wry smile. "Maybe we'll talk some more about those Spencers showing up so mysteriously in the hands of the Juáristas. Meantime, you are welcome to bunk in the bachelor officers' quarters and eat army chow. There's plenty of room, undermanned as we are. Also, turn your stock in with our mounts tonight inside the post."

Jesse thanked him without accepting and left, seeing now the friendly hand of Tom Ayers at work. Would he take the job? It was tempting because of the pay, yet he thought not. It meant more military service, likely more fighting, and he was overwhelmingly weary of war to the bottom of his being.

Early that afternoon, anticipating company, Jesse currycombed and brushed the red horse, saddled and tied him to a mesquite. Sure enough, not long afterward, Eleanor Ayers and another lady, riding sidesaddle, and Jamie on his spotted pony, rode up to Jesse's camp escorted by four troopers. Jesse was introduced to Mrs. Amelia Taylor, blue-eyed, blond curls showing under her pretty hat, in a riding habit of probably the latest style, and like her husband, a person of obvious spirit, Jesse discerned, some years younger than her spouse.

"We've come to see your copper-colored horse," Eleanor said. "When I told Mrs. Taylor that he once ran wild, a real mustang, she was just as anxious to see him."

"Pleased for you ladies to look him over." Jesse untied the horse and led him out for all to see.

"He does have the bold look you described," Eleanor said. "And I like the way he holds his head. He's so proud. He moves like a piece of silk."

"His blaze looks like spilled milk," said Mrs. Taylor. "How is he for traveling?"

"Has a nice running walk," Jesse explained. "There's an old saying about an easy-riding horse that goes, 'You could drink a cup of coffee on him and never spill a drop.' An exaggeration, but not too far off."

"I love his color," Eleanor enthused. Observing closer, she asked, "And the pretty red ribbon in his mane?"

"My late wife, Ana, did that."

"It's very pretty in his black mane," she said softly, her eyes lifting briefly to his white hair.

By now she knows. Jesse said no more.

Jaime dismounted, flung the pony's reins to Corporal Daly and marched up to the red horse. "May I pet him, sir?" Jaime was on his manners.

"Go ahead," Jesse said. "He won't mind."

The boy stretched to stroke the blazed face. The horse blew through his nostrils, but didn't back away.

Jaime flinched. "He acts a little wild. Can he run fast?"

"He can run fast for a long way."

"What's his name, sir?"

"El Soldado."

"What does that mean?"

"In Spanish, the Soldier. He's been in as many battles and skirmishes in Mexico as I have. He never bolts under gunfire."

"He is brave! Did you name him, Mr. Wilder?"

"No, Jaime. My wife did."

"Why isn't your wife here with you, Mr. Wilder?"

Before Jesse could answer, the boy's mother said sharply, "Jaime, you do not ask such personal questions. Where are your manners, young sir?"

Jaime hung his head. "I'm sorry, sir."

Jesse smiled at him forgivingly. "That's all right, son. I'm glad you asked about my wife. She was killed in Mexico when the French attacked our camp. I was gone. There were just a few Mexican patriots there to protect the women and children. One of the many sad things that can happen in war, Jaime, as your father the general knows."

"I'm sorry, Mr. Wilder."

Jesse patted the boy's shoulder.

"We should like to invite you to go riding with us, Mr. Wilder," Eleanor Ayers said at that needed moment.

He didn't hesitate. "Thank you. I'll be glad to go."

He mounted and posted himself to the left of the ladies, remembering that junior officers properly rode to the left of senior officers, in this case a brevet brigadier general's lady.

They rounded the fort and struck off southeast on the Butterfield Trail. Jaime and Corporal Daly brought up the rear, the boy belaboring the short-legged pony with heel kicks to maintain a trot.

"Jaime," his mother called back, "Patches is doing the best he can, trying to keep up with the horses. So we'll go at a slow trot. Don't punish him, you hear?"

"Yes, ma'am."

She turned to Jesse and, smiling, said conversationally, "The general is very excited about interviewing a citizen general who played a leading role in Mexico's recent war of liberation. He wants to write a history of it, and has been collecting material for some time. As you've probably gathered, he's a very determined man and will do what he says."

"I'm glad he is," Jesse said. "Otherwise, the true story would never be written. I mean what happened in Chihuahua. I can't speak for other Juárista forces, such as the one commanded by Diaz. I think President Juárez may face a troublesome strongman in Diaz, who they say has great ambition to rule Mexico like a dictator. There's still much for the general and me to discuss: training methods, tactics, deployment of cavalry in coordination with infantry, weapons, supplies. On and on."

"He would like very much for you to become the next civilian scout," she said, an inviting tone in her words.

"I do appreciate the offer."

"He hopes you will decide soon."

"One drawback is that I know nothing about this part of New Mexico, particularly the mountains."

"Is there a second reason?"

"The main one: I'm worn out with military service, although in all honesty I have to admit it's the only occupation I've known since 'sixty-one. The only one I've had time for."

"There are less attractive ways to live, Mr. Wilder. I realize that even more, and am thankful, when I see the thin immigrant women and the pinched faces of their children, in their eyes the hope they'll find a beautiful home somewhere, which I hope they do. And when I see the drifters that come to the post, some no doubt running from trouble back in the states, I am further thankful for the security the Army gives its people."

He nodded in acknowledgment.

They approached a clutter of huts, pens holding horses and mules, and a long adobe building with a store and saloon sign which Jesse had paid little attention to coming in with the escort and ox train.

A stout Anglo woman draped in a loose, ill-fitting red dress slouched in the doorway of the adobe, the pouches under her eyes heavy from sleep. She touched at her unkempt hair when she saw the troopers, the beginning of a smile working across her slack mouth.

"That dreadful place," Mrs. Taylor said to Jesse as they rode nearer. "The general calls it a hog ranch. It's off the military reservation or he would have it torn down. Many of the post's troubles start here. Cheap whiskey, lewd women, fights."

The woman was still smiling when they rode by. Two troopers traded knowing glances.

Time slipped by while the women chatted. The post shrank to a dark brown rectangle below the humping hills and imposing Cooke's Peak. Daly and another trooper struck up a long conversation. Without warning, Daly twisted around, shouting Jaime's name, and kicked his mount into a hard run.

Jaime was half a mile away, whipping the spotted pony at a lumbering run toward the hills.

"That boy!" his mother exclaimed.

Daly soon caught up. Grabbing the pony's bridle by the cheekpiece, he turned the pony around and back they came at a walk, Jaime slumped pouting in the saddle.

"Young man," Mrs. Taylor said when the two arrived, "you are close to being confined to quarters for a week. I ought to put you in the guardhouse on bread and water. What do you mean, running off like that?"

"I wanted to ride closer to the mountains."

"Never by yourself, you know that. And Corporal Daly, I think you ought to keep a much closer watch on Jaime."

"Yes, ma'am. I agree. I'm sorry. I got to talkin'."

"No excuse. I won't put you on report. But hereafter don't let him stray. He's fascinated with the mountains."

"Yes, ma'am!" He snapped her a most correct salute.

By then it was time to turn back. At the post, Jesse thanked the ladies and rode to camp, took the mule off picket and watered both animals at the spring before picketing them again.

He could not, he decided, accept the general's offer to bunk in the bachelor officers' quarters that night and turn his stock in with post mounts, when tomorrow he would decline the offer as scout.

It became a restless night for him as he considered his choices.

Serving again with people he knew and understood, even though they wore the once-detested Union blue, living within the bounds of discipline . . . might say, behind the shield of Army discipline . . . instead of giving in to vague wanderings and striking on west. He'd cheated death too many times to cringe when danger loomed, which it would as a civilian scout in Apache country. He'd reached the stage in life where death was almost an intellectual matter, rational instead of emotional. War taught a man what to fear and what not to fear, lest small fears confuse him and bring him down, blinding him to the main and possibly killing threat. A soldier feared excruciating pain more than sudden death—then it was over. Many people journeyed through life with only ordinary fears: being left alone as a child in darkness, missing a meal, getting a cold, going without water for half a day, damaging new clothes, being short of funds or late for church or without warm shelter at night, though fears for family and friends were certainly sensible and of grave concern.

Though time had eased his pain, what had happened in Mexico was constantly on his mind, as vivid as yesterday. But he realized more and more that he could bring nobody back and he had to get on with his life.

A surprising thought occurred to him. Maybe he needed to point himself in a new direction, away from shiftless wandering and what chance might toss his way. Not long ago he had left a just cause which he had helped bring to a successful conclusion. Maybe he needed another cause to right his life. The thought jarred him. Another cause? *God forbid!*

Seven

Colonel Taylor was impatiently waiting in the morning when Jesse went to headquarters after "Boots and Saddles" blew for Mounted Drill at eight o'clock, feeling not unlike a trooper reporting for duty.

"Overnight I thought of a barrage of questions," Taylor said, his crisp voice rising with enthusiasm. "First, let's go over the San Juan de Río fight again in more detail, in case I missed something. I know there are other particulars I failed to ask about, including more about Citizen General Floyd's role and Father Garza. I also want background on you and General Floyd: family, schooling, service in the Confederate Army, and such. As I envision it, a book could be done on your old outfit alone, the Army of Northern Chihuahua, just tying in what happened elsewhere. I already have a publisher in mind. A query will go off by the next mail East." He rubbed his hands. "Now for details, details. I am a stickler for details, General Wilder."

Jesse smiled. "Yes, sir, and I want you to have every detail."

Taylor yelled for an orderly to bring coffee and mugs.

They talked without letup until Guard Mount and Dismounted

Drill sounded at ten-thirty. Whereupon, Taylor looked up from his steady writing, a signal that the session was over.

"There's still a good deal to cover. Guess I'm just getting warmed up. Can you come back in the morning?"

Jesse nodded.

"Fine. Thank you." As they stood, Taylor added, "By now I hope you've had time to consider my offer as civilian scout and have decided to take it?"

"I've decided to decline the offer, General, with thanks."

Disregarding that with a little shake of his head, Taylor made a further dismissive gesture. "I understand your feelings, General Wilder, but it's way too early to decide after what you've just been through. Sleep on it some more, General."

Jesse felt like smiling over Taylor's laying on of *General*, as if that mattered anymore. "I've decided, sir. It's final."

Taylor pretended he hadn't heard. "And why haven't you moved your gear into the bachelor officers' quarters? You know you're welcome and to join the garrison at mess."

"But I'm not the civilian scout, General."

"You're not on your Southern manners, are you, General?"

"Not at all."

"Perhaps, then, you're just dodging Union cavalry cooking?"

"I did sample it at length on the Plains."

"That's it!" Taylor said, smacking his hands, and they both laughed. "Well, do as you like. When we get together again in the morning, perhaps you can tell me more about those Spencers."

"Very effective, sir. Very effective," knowing that wasn't what Taylor meant, but where they came from and how.

Jesse went to the post trader's store on one of the short sides of the rectangle and bought supplies, including some tinned food, pipe tobacco, matches, an extra blanket for the high-country nights, a *Century* magazine, and a bottle of Old Blue Grass bourbon, though he doubted that it would measure up to what Ayers had served so generously.

He was unpacking supplies, thinking what else he might need for his continuing westward odyssey after he and Taylor had finished their drawn-out discussions, when a trooper rattled up in a mule-drawn wagon. He waved, and unloaded a large sack of grain and a bale of hay, plus two armloads of pine firewood.

"What's this for?" Jesse asked, baffled.

"Compliments of the post," the soldier said. "You be General Wilder, I take it?"

Jesse nodded, amused at the additional inducing references to his former rank; however, his was as proper as Taylor's, permanent to boot, because Jesse's hadn't been brevet. Not that it mattered now.

He threw down hay for his stock and cleaned their feet with a hoofhook and checked their shoes, replaced at Mesilla. There he'd remembered to buy an extra set to carry along, a precaution learned from Yankee cavalrymen on the Plains, where shoes were changed every four weeks, whether needed or not, and mounts were groomed every morning and evening, except Sundays and holidays, and fed three times daily when on post. Daily care kept a solid horse under a man and was often the key to maintaining the scalp on his head.

A few other needed items, overlooked earlier, jogged his memory and he made a return trip to the post trader's store in the afternoon. Mulling over a drink, he was reminded it would be a good time to post a letter home, if he had someone to write to. His older brother, Claiborne, lived in Corinth, and his sister, Mary Elizabeth Somerville, also older, was in Lexington. Both had refused to include him in their father's estate at the family lawyer's suggestion. Both as unforgiving as their father was. *Fire-eating Claiborne, who never fired a shot while holding a major's commission with the government in Atlanta, and who'd fled to New Orleans when Atlanta fell. Claiborne, who as executor of the estate couldn't wait to get his hands on the old homeplace in the country and sell it cheap. The old farm, once a refuge of love and friendship, something to go back to, a symbol of when the Wilders were a family—now it was gone.*

He let his mind wander back, picturing Claiborne exuding hurt pride as he told an acquaintance, "I tell you, sir, our family was mighty hurt when Jesse chose to serve in the Yankee army out West," and the other man saying, "Seems to me he must have had ample reason—that or die in a hellhole Yankee prison camp," and Claiborne, puffing up, replying, "True, he was in a Yankee prison, but nothing warrants such dishonor, sir. Nothing! Absolutely nothing, sir!"

Fire-eating Claiborne, who never fired a shot.

But he would take pen in hand after all, for his one friend back there, that good man, gaunt and graying, Mr. B. L. Sawyer, the family attorney, who had interceded in Jesse's behalf without success and suggested that he contest the will, which Jesse had declined. He wrote:

Dear Mr. Sawyer,

Again, after a long and unavoidable delay, I want you to know my whereabouts. Today I am at Fort Cummings, which is on the old Butterfield Trail, in southwestern New Mexico, also in the heart of Apache country. Since I last wrote you from El Paso, I have fought with and helped train Mexican peasants in Chihuahua under the banner of President Benito Juárez. Our victory was complete, which you probably have read about, including the execution of Archduke Maximilian, which I protested to no avail.

Otherwise, it was a just war and one cause in which we ex-Confederates played a major part and clearly won.

My plans are to continue west from here. My health is good, and as a Tennesseean you will be pleased to know that I ride a good horse, a once-wild mustang the color of the sun.

I thank you again, sir, for your efforts in my behalf and I trust this will find you in good health.

Sincerely, Jesse Alden Wilder

Just penning the letter, just retaining a connection back home, gave him a better feeling and diminished his resentment. Loss of family hurt most of all, most of all his father, because Jesse and Claiborne, a spoiled first son, had never been close, and his sister, married at sixteen, was gone from home during his growing-up years. His dear mother had died before the war. As for his dispossession, he could contribute it only to unforgiving Southern pride, kindled by defeat.

That evening he enjoyed the ease of a quick pinewood fire at supper, instead of having to forage for fuel with a hand ax among the tough mesquites. Summer's twilight lingered past eight o'clock, and when darkness crept in, he sat for a long time, smoking and watching his pungent, friendly fire. As soon as he and the general were finished talking, in another day or so, he would saddle up and go.

It was late when he turned in, and even then sleep eluded him for a while, kept awake by his inner restlessness. Arizona, California? What then?

Later, much later, something broke his sleep. He listened, his usual guardedness growing. He caught it again. A foreign intrusion across the otherwise still night, but it didn't seem near. Sound traveled far in the thin air of the arid high country. Something far off could sound closer than it was. This seemed distant, he judged, but not way off . . . coming from beyond the post, from the east . . . nearer now.

By habit, he reached for the carbine and sat up, aware only of puzzlement, no alarm. The sound had faded, the night was silent now. His horse, close by, had quit grazing and was watching as well.

Then he heard it again, definitely nearer. A familiar sound or sounds—the rattle and rumble of wagons over rough ground—heavy wagons. He set himself to reasoning. It was unlikely that immigrants would be traveling at night. On further thought, not a bad idea in Apache country, inasmuch as it was said Apaches didn't attack at night. He had never experienced a night attack, a theory still up for question until one occurred. There was a difference now in the sounds. When first heard, he realized suddenly, they'd come from the north or northeast—from the direction of the mountains —not along the east-going immigrant trail.

He pulled on trousers and boots and started walking back along the trail, the Spencer in hand. Passing the post, he heard sentries calling, "Four o'clock and all's well," which brought up another possibility, which he quickly dismissed. Army wagons traveling east at night would have left the post far earlier if the plan was to avoid Apaches. In the first place, the wagons hadn't come from the fort.

As he walked, nothing changed. The sounds had quit and he began to wonder where the wagons had gone, unless eastward. He kept going, questioning what could get him out of his blankets at this early hour. More than curiosity was drawing him on, instead a gathering sense of contradiction. Roaming clouds let moon haze filter through. The deep-rutted trail guided him. But still no wagon racket.

He must have covered a mile beyond the post when he topped a rise and saw a yellow splash of light breaking the murk, and light moving away from it, the bobbing of lantern light. The location had to be the hog ranch of Mrs. Taylor's graphic description.

He walked faster, picking up muffled voices and, more distinct, harness and chain sounds, but no creaking wagons. He took that to mean teams were being changed or watered. Nearer, he made out the dingy shapes of three hooded wagons parked in front of the adobe and the movements of several riders. Light inside the adobe outlined a man standing in the doorway.

Jesse halted. A man carrying a lantern came from behind the adobe and spoke to the man in the doorway. They talked briefly, the faint drift of that to Jesse sounding like Spanish, and then the man with the lantern went inside and the one in the doorway closed the door behind them. The riders dismounted, but did not go inside. Presently, he smelled tobacco smoke.

The sky was beginning to change to a grayish shade. Before long the riders could see him. It was time to go back. Still, he delayed, watching the sprawling layout materialize in the new light, curious to look in the stock pens behind the adobe. But a man could get shot damned quick snooping around somebody's horses and mules.

The light was still burning in the adobe when he turned back, trying to piece the bits of this together. Coming from the mountains, the wagons couldn't belong to immigrants—that was plain. Maybe miners who'd struck it rich leaving the country, traveling at night for safety? But generally you didn't change teams at four o'clock in the morning, and you didn't rout a man out of bed at that hour to do so. He guessed he'd acquired a downright suspicious mind since the ambushed Benedict train, and the horror frozen on Junius Russell's face and the strange voice the Texan said he'd heard, and the golden-haired woman and her little boy. Brutality that had to be seen to be believed. Now part of the everlasting pall over the mind of a man who'd seen too much.

One of Father Alberto's many reflections occurred to him as he walked on. *God chose you for what you've experienced because you're strong enough to bear it.* Jesse could only wonder and doubt.

He cleared his mind. He would see Tom Ayers first thing in the morning. Something, he sensed, at least a looking-into, ought to be done.

He watered and fed his stock, put them on picket, cooked breakfast, and when stable call sounded at six o'clock, he saddled the red horse and rode to the fort.

He found the lieutenant at the stables, conversing with a sergeant over the care of a lame horse. "You're up early, sir," Ayers said. "What brings you out?"

Jesse led him aside and sketched in everything, from hearing the wagons to seeing them parked at the adobe, and the sounds of changing teams, and the waiting riders and the confab in the adobe.

"I didn't hear a thing," Ayers said.

"Because you're closed in. At first, I thought it was travel on the trail, but soon realized it wasn't—that got me up. Something doesn't fit. Strange. After what you and I've been thorough lately, I'm getting suspicious of anything that's out of the usual."

"More than a little unusual that time of night, I agree."

"Suppose a detail could pay a call at the hog ranch?"

"We'd better take this to the Old Man." Ayers rubbed his jaw. "Lord, Jesse, you are getting my curiosity aroused!"

At headquarters Colonel Taylor was lending an ear to the harried officer of the day, who was telling his CO that a fight between the wives of two noncommissioned officers who served as laundresses had upset the calm of the post.

"What shall I do, sir?" the OD asked. "I've never had to settle a matter like this before."

"Here's a piece of well-established advice, Lieutenant. Since women are the same the world over, remember never try to referee a fight between 'em. It's too dangerous for the referee. So just pass the word to their husbands to calm things down."

"Thank you, sir. I'll pass the word."

As the officer left, Taylor turned to the two waiting. "This laundry situation causes as much trouble as that blasted hog ranch."

"That's part of what Mr. Wilder and I feel should be brought to your attention, General," Ayers said. "He can explain it better than I can."

Jesse went through his report as before, concluding, "Things don't fit. Wagons coming out of the mountains at night. Changing teams at four in the morning. After what we've seen lately, I'm suspicious of anything out of the ordinary."

"It is out of the usual order of things," Taylor said. "But you haven't said what you think all this means."

"It's just suspicious, sir. Strange as hell. Why all this at night?"

Taylor folded his arms, speaking while he paced back and forth. "I've been wanting to close that pest hole ever since I was posted here. But since it's off the military reservation, there's nothing we can do legally. If we shut him down, the proprietor there . . . What's his name, Mr. Ayers?"

"Jacob Vane."

". . . would raise a howl that could be heard as far as Washington. I've been told that through certain business contacts he also has powerful political connections." He halted and faced about. "What's always been a mystery to me is why an entrepreneur—if I may dishonor the word—would set up a business way out here in Apache country, when he could make a comfortable living, say, in Mesilla or Las Cruces or El Paso, or in the mountain mining camps. How could he make more here off our cash-poor troopers and the poor, passing immigrants with his degenerate women, rotgut whiskey, and crooked games than he could elsewhere? Which leads to a logical assumption. He has other ways of turning a good profit. Ways that strain the imagination. However, I am forgetting that, besides the saloon, he does run a little store—groceries and supplies. What do you think, Mr. Ayers?"

"I think we should have a talk with Mr. Vane."

"About what? We can't just bust in there and ask what was going on last night. He could claim harassment and intimidation by the Army, which is about as popular now in Washington as a skunk at a Sunday School picnic, with Congress and the Benzine Boards bent on cutting us down, not only to the bone, but to the marrow."

"We could say we're looking for missing government property."

"Such as . . . ?"

"Horses, mules, carbines, saddles."

"Mmnn. And you, Mr. Wilder?"

"Those three wagons could carry something of interest."

"Such as . . . ? Be specific. Give me some details."

"Goods. People who travel only at night are usually trying to hide something. There was a great deal of smuggling going on across the border in and below El Paso when I was in Chihuahua. Yet you wouldn't expect smuggled goods to come out of the mountains."

"Who knows all that's in those mountains, and it's not many miles from here to the border. Wide open all the way." Taylor made a nervous motion with his right arm, which, Jesse remembered from their long talks, meant he had come to a snap decision. "That's it! I've been looking for an excuse—any kind, thin as it is. You will be looking for contraband intended for Mexico. Goods prohibited by law from being exported. Contraband and missing government property. . . . Mr. Ayers, you will form the usual detail immediately and ride to the hog ranch. If the wagons are still there, inform Jacob Vane of your purpose and search them. Also his stock pens, just in case there's anything bearing a U.S. brand, and look about the premises, just in case there's a stray army carbine about. Tell him some weapons are missing from our armory. . . . If the wagons are gone, then Vane will have to come forth. If he refuses, tell him we'll close him down, whether he's off the reservation or not, for interfering with military operations. However, I can't see him totally refusing. He'll make a pretense, at least. If you find any government property on the premises, arrest him on the spot and bring him in."

Taylor struck the nervous motion again. "If he cooperates and tells you where the wagons went, pursue until you find 'em. Stop and search. Use force, if necessary. If everything is on the up-and-up, the wagon people shouldn't object to being searched. In that case, and all is well, doff your hat with apologies. Better plan on rations for three days. Take Sergeant Tim O'Grady."

He stopped, his mouth firming, the signal for dismissal.

Eight

Sergeant Tim O'Grady called the detail to attention.

"Detail formed, sor."

"Prepare to mount," Ayers said. "Mount!"

Leather squealed as the detail hit the saddles.

"Right by twos—harch!"

They swung out of the post at an extended trot, Ayers leading a detail of eight troopers. Jesse rode with the Blakeslee cartridge box tied to the saddlehorn and the Spencer fully loaded, seven shots in the magazine and one in the chamber. His mule and gear he'd left in the fort.

Some distance past the fort, less than it had seemed to Jesse when walking the trail in darkness, they topped the rise from which he had first sighted the light in the adobe and the moving lantern.

He looked and said, "The wagons are gone, Lieutenant. They must have been in a hurry, pulled out before sunup."

They clattered up to the adobe and dismounted. The coarse-looking woman Jesse recalled seeing while riding with the ladies seemed to appear as if by magic, a suggestive smile playing along her heavy mouth as she eyed the troopers one by one. Her expression changed when Ayers told her, "We're here to see Mr. Jacob Vane."

"What you want?"

"I'll talk to him, not you."

He went to the door, Jesse a step behind, holding the carbine down in one hand.

A voice called from inside, "Who is it, Millie?"

"Some soldiers."

"Show 'em in, of course."

She flounced away and gestured to a cramped, low-ceilinged room that held a battered bar and rough tables and chairs. From a room behind the bar emerged a bush-bearded, slope-shouldered man, his jowly smile on Ayers. Grease spotted the shirtfront over his watermelon-shaped paunch. He gave the immediate effect of the easy cordiality of the frontier host, but behind the cynical eyes in the domelike head stirred a quick wariness.

"The Army's always welcome for a drink on the house," he said, waving a thick arm. "What'll you gentlemen have?"

Ayers declined with a shake of his head. "I'm Lieutenant Ayers. This is Mr. Wilder. We're here to ask you about possible contraband in three wagons that stopped here a few hours after midnight."

Vane stood back, looking aghast. "Contraband in wagons?"

"Yes, sir. Wagons observed around four o'clock or soon after. They came from the mountains. The Army has reason to suspect they might have carried contraband headed for Mexico."

"What kind of contraband?"

"There could be many kinds, from guns to trade goods."

Vane leaned against the bar, lifting both hands in a who-me? gesture. "Sure, some wagons pulled in here. I didn't see 'em come in. First thing I knew was somebody poundin' on the door. They got me outa bed. But I didn't look in the wagons. Why would I? This is no border station. I have no idea what they carried. But I will say this, if they came from the mountains, like you say, that's the last place a man'd think of as a source for contraband."

"On the other hand," Ayers countered, "a good and unexpected place to hide contraband."

Vane shrugged an indifferent shoulder.

"Did they change teams?" Ayers asked.

"No."

Vane was becoming less and less communicative.

"If they didn't change teams, sir, why was it necessary to get you out of bed at that hour?"

Vane eased. "Lieutenant, I see you don't savvy civilian teamsters. One thing, in fact, first thing they wanted was water for their mules. I haul water from the big spring, you know; it's for everybody. Not just the Army. I've dug me a tank out back for the convenience of folks passin' through, or anybody that needs stock water. A public service. Next thing the teamsters wanted was whiskey. A teamster's got to have his whiskey, you ought to know. Plenty of it. Keeps him goin'."

"Where did they go from here, Mr. Vane?"

"They didn't say and I didn't ask. I went back to bed as soon as I'd rustled up some whiskey. They paid me."

The lieutenant's politeness took on an edge. "It strikes me as reasonable that you could determine by the racket the wagons made when pulling out which direction they took—either east on the trail or south for Mexico."

Vane shifted his feet. "I'd like to oblige you, Lieutenant, but the wagons were still here when I went back to bed. I could still hear the teamsters talkin' over their drinks when I dropped off to sleep. I'd say they's headed for Mesilla—that's my guess."

"I see. Can you tell me why they were traveling that late at night? Did they say?"

Vane's voice struck a brittle note. "I don't ask everybody that stops here what their business is. Wouldn't be healthy sometimes, if you get what I mean? Some rough *hombres* travel this trail on the dodge, and I never ask what their name was back in the states. But I'd say the main reason they's travelin' at night was to avoid Apaches. Too, night travel's easier on mules."

"That's logical, Mr. Vane. Very logical. Now, sir, for the second purpose of our call. With all due courtesy, we ask permission to search the premises for any government equipment that might have inadvertently found its way here."

The last of Vane's cordiality vanished. "Search my place!" he exploded. "Where's your god-damned warrant?"

At the sound of his voice a muscular white man stepped to the entrance of the room behind the bar, a man big enough to fill the doorway.

Jesse shifted the carbine into both hands.

Seeing that, Vane made a checking gesture and the man didn't move past the doorway. Calming down, Vane said, "I remind you that I'm a United States citizen and I believe it's customary to show a warrant before a man's house or business is searched. Furthermore, my establishment is not on the military reservation."

"You have nothing to fear, Mr. Vane," Ayers said in a level tone, "if there is no government property here. As for a warrant, sir, I am acting on an order from the post commander, which is warrant enough in this vicinity, even off the reservation, because the search involves U.S. property. Moreover, I point out to you that if the contract surgeon at the post ever traces one dose of the clap to your so-called establishment, you'll be closed down in five minutes, this place nailed shut." Ayers turned and called, "Sergeant O'Grady—in here!"

A ruddy-faced, mustached O'Grady appeared on the double, carbine in hand. "Yes, sor!"

"Take six men and search the building," Ayers ordered. "You know what to look for."

Vane did not protest. He leaned against the bar, arms folded, showing a suffering expression while the troopers went through room after room.

A woman's high-pitched voice, screaming a torrent of curses, erupted at one end of the adobe.

Soon after that O'Grady reported, more red of face. "Millie ran us out of her room, sor, but there wasn't nothin' in there but a busted bed and some quilts and a chamber pot."

"Very good, Sergeant."

"Everything else is clear, sor."

"May talk to you later, Mr. Vane," Ayers said. "Now we'll look into the outbuildings."

"I really didn't expect to find any carbines in the main building," Ayers said to Jesse when they were outside. "He's smarter than that. But I wanted him to know that we suspect him of anything, and that we'll search whenever we please. He knows damn well where the wagons were headed. He let drop Mesilla, like a good guess, but I don't believe him. More likely that was to mislead us. He's never obliged the Army in any way, which is all the more reason to doubt

Mesilla. Yet he profits from us. I dread to report back to the Old Man that Vane did not come forth with more reliable information."

"We're not through looking yet," Jesse said, "and you could still threaten to arrest and jail him."

"I don't think the Old Man wants to go that far unless we find something here. As is, we're left with two possible routes, sticking to the contraband theory. They could have gone southwest, aiming for Janos, to pick up the trail that runs between the Santa Rita copper mines and Chihuahua. We understand up here that Janos is a big smuggling center in northern Chihuahua. The copper smelters are farther south. The other choice is to avoid Cooke's Canyon and go northwest from the Santa Rita Trail, picking up the Butterfield into Arizona, then dropping down to the Sonoran border at Agua Prieta or Nogales. But that route seems too far out of the way for smuggling from this part of the country."

He stopped to tell O'Grady, "You men search the sheds," and walked on with Jesse toward two adobe huts.

A very young Mexican girl, slim and pretty, stood watching in the doorway of the first hut.

Jesse touched the rim of his hat to her and spoke in his somewhat awkward Spanish, *"Señorita,* did you see the wagons that stopped here early this morning?"

"They woke me up, *señor.* I saw them, yes." Her black eyes were like great bruises in the doll-like face. She was so slight that he could have been talking to a child.

"Did you hear the teamsters say where they were going?"

The black eyes cut to the corner of the adobe, where Vane now stood, watching her.

Seeing her fear, Jesse thought she couldn't be a day over fourteen and wondered where Vane had got her. Maybe bought her. Probably El Paso or across the river at El Paso del Norte. The hut was no more than a prostitute's crib, common in Mexico City's slums.

She started to speak, seemed to reconsider. As if choosing her words, she said, "The wagons very noisy, yes. Too noisy to hear men talking, *señor.*"

"Did one of the teamsters come to see you and did you talk to him? Yes?"

"Oh, no, *señor.*" She was hurrying now, in evident fear, still watching Vane. "I no talk to anybody." With that, she went inside and closed the door.

"*Señorita,* listen to me. Which way did the wagons go from here? It is important that we know."

She didn't answer.

"She knows more than she let on," Jesse said, going with Ayers toward the second hut.

Ayers kicked a loose rock. "Vane's got her too scared to talk."

An aging Anglo woman was waiting for them, a languid hand carelessly on her right hip. Even at this early hour her slack mouth was painted, and she had powdered the pouches under her eyes. Her brownish hair was as tangled as a bird's nest.

"Guess it's my turn," Ayers said low to Jesse. He tipped his hat to her and made an elaborate bow. "Ma'am, did you see the wagons that came in not long before sunup?"

"How could I miss 'em? They woke me up."

"We're trying to determine the direction they took from here. Can you tell us?"

"That bunch was in a hurry, I tell you," she said, a scoffing in her strident voice. "Wouldn't stop long enough for a little fun."

"Then you conversed with them?"

"Y'mean talk? Hell, yes, I talked to 'em—well, to one. But like I said, he was in a hurry. How's a girl gonna make a livin' way out here with men like that?"

Ayers nodded in understanding. "Did he happen to tell you what the wagons carried?"

"I didn't look in the wagons, soldier boy. No call to."

"Did the man you talked to tell you where the wagons were going?"

"No call for him to tell me, a stranger, and no call for me, a stranger, to stick my nose in. What did that matter? By that time he was already in a hurry to get along."

"Which way did they go when they pulled out?"

"You know, I don't even remember. By then I was all tucked in and sleepin' like a babe in my sainted mother's arms. You better ask Mr. Vane, soldier boy. He knows what goes on around here at all hours."

Money talks, Jesse thought. He decided to challenge her. "Would a dollar or two spark your memory about where the wagons went?"

Her face didn't alter. "Not even a dollar or two," she said, "and a dollar's a dollar out here, in a land that God forgot he ever made, if he did."

For a split second he felt the despair and resignation lacing her words. Then she seemed to find a rough animation. She looked squarely at Ayers, and at Jesse, judging them. "How about you, boys? Got time for a little old-time fun on the run?"

Ayers flushed and Jesse grinned at his discomfort.

"Happens we're in a hurry, too," Ayers said, and with a touch of his hat, took his mannerly leave.

"She knows where the wagons went," Jesse said.

"Let's take a look at the stock," Ayers said.

Horses and mules milled in the main corral. Jesse studied them. "Four mules show sweat and harness marks as fresh as a few hours ago," he said. "So at least one wagon changed teams."

"They look like the big Missouri breed to me."

"They do. Not that that tells us anything. There must be a lot of Missouri mules used on the trail."

Sergeant O'Grady reported. "Nothing in the sheds, Lieutenant, but a few goats."

"All right, Sergeant. Keep the detail formed out front while Mr. Wilder and I look around." And to Jesse, "There are wagon tracks trailing off everywhere."

Jesse was strolling around the pen, trying to make something of the maze of wagon tracks, when he noticed an old Mexican man watching him from a feed shed. He continued to watch Jesse and did not eye the adobe in fear as had the Mexican girl and the woman.

Jesse glanced back. Vane was no longer there. Going on, he saw several sets of broad wagon tracks angling off from around the corral. Fresh tracks. He bent down. The sides of the tracks were beginning to crumble slightly from the sun. Manure droppings were just starting to dry. He followed the tracks out about fifty yards and back. The old man was still watching him.

Jesse went over to him. Vane had not returned to the corner of the adobe. "Good morning, *señor*," Jesse greeted him in Spanish. "These are tough times, eh?"

"Very tough, *señor*. I miss my Mexico, hard as times are there. Only there you have family and friends, fiestas and holy days."

"What do you do here?"

"I feed and care for the stock. I am good with stock."

"I'll bet you are."

"But things are not as they were promised."

"Why can't you go home?"

No answer. Fear in that silence.

"You have no friends here?"

"Only the poor child in the hut."

Jesse nodded that he understood and passed a silver dollar into the old man's hand. "Maybe this will help a little."

The old man's black eyes were suddenly wet. *"Gracias, señor. Gracias."*

"Before daylight this morning," Jesse said, "some wagons rolled in here from the mountains. Whiskey was bought and one wagon changed teams. The wagon people were in a big hurry. I would like to know where those wagons went, *señor*. I saw those big wagon tracks going southwest. Are those last night's wagons and where were they going, my friend?"

This time the old man glanced toward the adobe. Vane had not returned, apparently thinking the Mexican would not talk. But, still, the old man didn't speak. Instead, he pursed his mouth to the southwest in the direction of the tracks.

"To Janos?" Jesse asked softly.

The old man scarcely nodded, but he did nod. Then he turned and walked behind the shed.

Ayers was pondering over the tracks when Jesse came up. "You were right," Jesse said. "Vane was trying to mislead us to take the trail to Mesilla. The wagons are headed for Janos."

Ayers jerked around.

"I don't think we should jump Vane about it, as much we'd like to tell him we know he lied. If we do, he'll know somebody spilled the beans, likely the old Mexican, who has enough troubles, or the girl."

"We'll ride back as if going to the post," Ayers agreed. "When we reach the other side of the rise, turn southwest. I figure the wagons have a four- or five-hour start on us."

Vane watched from the adobe as the troopers left.

The detail picked up fresh wagon tracks not long after striking off to the southwest.

"They're heading for the Santa Rita–Janos Trail, all right," Ayers observed. "Interesting how well traveled this looks. Virtually a little trail itself from Vane's place, proof of the obvious: wagons leaving Vane's come this way now and then. Often enough to break out a trail. Surprising, and suspicious. Anything linked to him is."

Jesse reined off, examining the pattern of horse tracks parallel to the wagon trail. "Trying to figure out about how many riders in the party." He crossed to the other side of the trail, saying finally, "I'd say six to eight riders, Lieutenant. Makes a man think they aim to protect what they got."

The Santa Rita–Janos Trail turned out to be more of a road, Jesse saw as the morning drew on, a broad, rutted trace running north and south, showing few signs of recent passage except where the tracks from Vane's joined and turned south.

While everyone was eyeing the tracks, Jesse said, "On the Plains we figured a good cavalry mount could keep up a steady four miles an hour. What would you say, Lieutenant, four stout mules would make pulling a loaded wagon?"

"Depending on the load, about the same, or less. But keeping it up all day. In fact, at the end of a day outdoing a horse."

"Which puts us about twelve to sixteen miles behind the wagons, or a little less."

"Or a little more," Ayers said worriedly, and moved the detail out at an extended trot.

The morning faded into layers of shimmering white heat, and early afternoon found the detail's sights on the jagged peaks of the Florida Mountains, floating like islands on the ocean of desert.

Coming to the Mimbres River, Ayers ordered a halt. "We've been moving faster than your four miles an hour, so we'll rest a short while. How do you see this, Captain?"

"We know we're on the right track."

Ayers filled a stubby pipe. "Or should I address you as general?" he asked, with a touch of good-natured banter.

"Jesse will do. Also forget the captain."

"I'm glad you're along, a man of your experience. Which reminds me. Here you are doing the work of a government scout, but you're not getting paid for it."

"I had my chance and turned it down. Guess I don't want to be tied down. But I'm as interested in those wagons as anybody."

"You could have ridden away from this, not been involved."

"And never find out what it was all about? Gets back to that curious animal, man. Since I started the fuss about the wagons, I want to hang around till we do find out."

"When do you think we'll catch up?"

"Before sundown, unless the wagon mules are the get of Pegasus. They have to rest, too."

"Getting back to the scout's job, I still think you ought to take it."

"Like I said, one thing, I don't know the country."

"I have to contradict you. You're learning it right now. In addition to having been over the trail from Mesilla to the post."

They trotted on. Afternoon heat closed in like a clamp. The condensed smell of sweaty horseflesh and fuming grayish dust hung about them in the dry air. The troopers said little. The realization registered on Jesse that again he was part of this way of life, something long familiar and again finding it energizing and keen. Comfort was a matter of shutting out certain conditions and savoring others.

Now the Floridas rose to the detail's left, their shadows inviting. Ayers halted for ten minutes, then moved on. The pace picked up after the rest, but soon settled to a dogged pursuit. For a long while they rode like this, the fresh prints of the wagons ever drawing them on. Now and then Ayers uncased field glasses to scan the distances.

It was short of late afternoon when, glasses raised, he said, "There they are!" and flung up a halting hand.

Jesse had to look again before he found the low smudge of crawling dust. In moments, through that haze, he made out the shapes of three hooded wagons, beside them the dark, sticklike figures of horsemen.

Ayers took the detail on at a faster clip.

Not until the troopers drew within about half a mile did the riders appear to discover pursuit. They stopped and came together while the wagons continued ahead. A parley seemed to be going on among the horsemen.

Suddenly the wagons halted.

A rider waved them to go on. He and the other riders fanned out.

"Six riders," Ayers said, checking the detail. "Looks like they're forming a rear guard."

"We'd better figure in the teamsters, too," Jesse said, "and they could have guards riding in the wagons."

"By now they know we're U.S. If they have nothing to hide, why fight us? But they're going to fight. Well, I know my orders, sir. Stop and search. Use force if necessary. That's one thing about the Old Man. He never sends you out with half-assed orders. And he's always instructed junior officers to use their own resources. Same as he did at Kelly's Ford." The lieutenant turned to the detail in column of twos. "We're going to form a front and proceed at a trot. Don't fire unless we're fired on. In that case, wait till I fire. As we advance, form on me. Don't bunch up. Space yourselves well."

He gave the command and the troopers spread out. Jesse checked his Spencer, fully loaded since morning, an eighth shell in the chamber, adjusted the sights and eared back the hammer.

"Lieutenant," he said, "the moment they open up, I'll keep up a steady fire, concentrating on the middle riders. That way, I think we can break up that front damn quick. I'd like to get in closer, within two hundred yards, if we can."

Hardly had he spoken when a rifle cracked, followed by a burst of shots from the riders.

When Ayers fired, the troopers started firing.

Jesse bided his time, not liking the range.

Blooms of powdersmoke marked the position of the rear guard. Jesse caught the humming of bullets overhead. Behind the riders the teamsters were frantically whipping the mule teams.

Jesse put two shots into the middle horsemen. Nothing happened. He raised the sights. His next bullet found a rider. The man lost his rifle and, slumping, rode toward the wagons a short way and dropped to the ground. Jesse began firing faster. A rider spilled from the saddle. Another fell, but his foot hung in a stirrup and the horse bolted, racing in a circle, dragging the hapless rider till he tore free.

To Jesse's right, a trooper pulled rein abruptly, clutching a shoulder.

A gray horse in the rear guard broke down, one foreleg dangling. Its dismounted rider ran for the wagons, but trooper fire knocked him down. The remaining two riders slanted away, racing not to protect the wagons, but to the west, toward a line of rocky hills.

Jesse emptied the carbine at them, but they were soon out of range. With practiced motions, he snapped open the cover plate in the carbine's buttstock, drew out the magazine and, holding it left-handed, took a tube of cartridges from the Quickloader. Sliding the shells into the buttstock magazine, he inserted the spring-loaded magazine tube, locked the cover plate and put back the empty tube in the Quickloader.

All this time the red horse had trotted steadily ahead, flinching at the carbine's first shots so close to his pricked ears, but showing no tendency to bolt or buck. A battlefield horse.

Earing back the hammer for each shot, Jesse now concentrated his fire on the lead wagon. For some moments there was no change, and then the wagon stopped. The other teamsters cut around and rushed ahead, lashing the teams.

Jesse heard Ayers shout, "Cut off those wagons—charge!" and the line of troopers pounded away, the wounded man following, holding his mount to a walk.

The red horse needed no urging to run. Riding beside Ayers, Jesse saw they were closing fast on the nearest wagon. A trooper on a fast chestnut, charging in from the end of the line, which gave him an angle, raced up alongside the trailing wagon. A rifleman leaned out from the wagon seat. A slash of sound. Smoke puffed. The trooper reeled, but hung on.

Ayers snapped off shots with his revolver. All at once the rifleman in the wagon jerked and half stood, trying to grab a wagon bow. He clutched, missed, lost his balance and, with a high scream, toppled from the seat, the wagon bumping as the right front wheel passed over him. The teamster eased up at once, jabbering in Spanish, trying to hold the four mules and raise his hands at the same time.

The other wagon hadn't slowed. But as the detail caught up, the guard threw up his hands and the teamster pulled in the mules. The fight was over.

"Get down," Ayers ordered the pair.

"Señor comandante," the teamster shouted, rushing his words, "this *hombre* he make me go on. I am a farmer on the Mimbres River like Juan—back there—hired to drive the mules. I have no gun. I hurt nobody."

The guard said no word, just grinned sheepishly. He was a wiry little whippet of a white man. A kind of shrewd grin spread on his whiskered face under the slouch hat pulled down around his jug-handle ears as he obligingly surrendered his rifle to Sergeant O'Grady. Something about his owlish face struck a vague response in Jesse's memory, erased when Ayers ordered the two and the other teamster marched back under guard and the wagons brought together.

"And now," the lieutenant said, "where's the rest of this outfit that was so eager to fight? I'll say this, Jesse, you know how to use that repeater. You worked the trigger guard like a pump handle. Your fast, sustained fire was a factor in breaking their front so soon."

"I've had a lot of practice. But I wasn't the only one firing. Two riders in the rear guard skedaddled. The rest look done for."

"Another burying detail," Ayers groaned as he scanned the field. "My, how I weary of it. I'm most curious as to who these people are and why they're here."

Leading their mounts, they walked back. The wounded gray horse, standing head down, leg dangling, took Jesse's eye. He crossed over and put the gray down with a shot to the head.

They came to the rifleman Ayers had shot, the man who fell under the wagon wheel. A white man of uncertain age, shaggy-haired as a buffalo hunter, with a dirty beard that covered most of his hawkish face. A border type, Jesse thought, hard as flint. Farther on, they found another man, this one lying facedown, the gray's rider, judging by his location. Jesse turned him over with the toe of his boot. The dead man was a Mexican of perhaps middle years, a great silver buckle on his belt, the spurs on his boots with large rowels.

At what had been the lead wagon, they found a dead teamster, a nondescript white man, slumped across the seat, and a dead guard, another white man, wedged between the seat and the front of the wagon. Not far from that wagon, on the road, still another white man.

"But no," Ayers said, "it's an Indian dressed like a white man. What tribe do you think he might be?"

"Anything but an Apache," Jesse said. "No braids. Means he's run with bad white men a long time."

On the road where the action had begun, they found another Indian, this one with braids.

"Could be the same tribe as the one that tried to steal my horse," Jesse said. "Whatever that might be."

Nearby lay a young white man, his sharp features and staring eyes reflective of wildness even in death. A Bowie knife and six-shooter at his belt of silver conchas and a Sharps rifle by an outflung hand. Wearing a broad sombrero with a leather chin strap, a red-checkered shirt, britches with silver buttons down the seams. High-heeled, black leather boots of fancy Mexican make.

"Young and wild, guess he gravitated toward bad company and found it—too bad," Jesse said, feeling only the old, dull weariness, thinking the young man was probably one of the first he'd knocked down in the rear guard.

"What do these men tell us?" Ayers wondered aloud.

"A mixed bunch of renegades, though the Indians surprise me. The wagons may tell us more."

As they started back, O'Grady ran up. "Sor, Corporal Casey's shot bad. Mulvane looks like he'll make it. He's still on his feet."

They hurried over to the wounded. Mulvane was standing, one hand favoring a bloody shoulder. Casey lay heaving. He'd taken a bullet in the chest. Ayers opened Casey's bloody jacket and shirt, looked and bit his lip.

"Let's take off his jacket, tear off a shirt sleeve and wrap his chest," Jesse suggested.

That done, Jesse took a bottle of tequila from his saddle pack, uncorked it and held it to Casey's lips. "Take a big swallow of this Mexican tonic, Corporal. You'll feel a heap better."

Casey did, and a weak grin floated across his pale ruddiness. "Never thought tequila'd taste so good. But it does."

Jesse then handed the bottle to Mulvane. "You men share this. It'll help a little. When you hurt till you can't stand it, take a slug."

"We'll put the boys in a wagon as soon as we see what the cargo is," Ayers said. "Sergeant O'Grady, get another man to hold the mules. Meantime, gather up any loose horses and get ready for the burial detail. Let's get along. Tonight, we'll camp in the Floridas."

Ayers let down the tailgate of the nearest wagon and climbed in, while Jesse watched. A tarpaulin covered the load to the top of the bows. Ayers tore back the canvas and stared. Before him stood orderly stacks of saddles, harness, horse collars, bridles, nose bags and saddle blankets.

"Mind seeing up front, Jesse? If it's the same as here, this load is worth some thousands of dollars. I don't see any McClellans—just civilian saddles. Nothing brand new. But looks in good shape."

Jesse climbed over the wagon wheel, drew the canvas cover aside and ranged his eyes over the stacks. "About the same up here," he called. "Some saddle bags. All look used. But good stuff."

They moved to another wagon. Ayers said, "Look," pointing to the weathered lettering in black on the wagon's side—THE MOLINE WAGON COMPANY—against the faded red, white and blue colors.

They didn't pause. As Ayers climbed in and pulled back the canvas, Jesse saw stacks of rifles, carbines, shotguns, open boxes of revolvers, boxes of percussion caps, cartridge boxes and a small barrel of powder. Jesse jumped up beside Ayers to see better. He picked up a carbine. "This is an old Burnside. . . . There's a Ballard. . . . Here's an old Starr carbine. An Enfield rifle. . . . This is a Mississippi rifle. Haven't seen one of these since 'sixty-one. . . . Here's a flat-framed Dance revolver, Southern-made and no recoil shield behind the cylinder. I wouldn't carry one. Some of these weapons look worn out. But anything that shoots has a market in northern Mexico, needed in the never-ending war with the Apaches. The Juáristas were buying poorer ordnance than this to use against the French when I joined them."

Ayers shifted his attention from the pile of weapons to Jesse, an easy bantering behind his eyes. "You mean they were able to get better arms after you and your friend joined, including the Spencers you told the Old Man about?"

The old caution was still upon Jesse. His face straight, he said,

"In one skirmish, Father Alberto happened to see what my one Spencer could do. He was impressed with the rate of fire. He had to have some. After that, somehow, enough Spencers for two companies showed up in camp. A great improvement over what the Juáristas had been using, and for the first time they could pour a sustained fire at the enemy. For certain, a deadly shock to the French, friend Tom."

They made for the last wagon, looking at the mules as they passed. "These are big mules with the wagons," Jesse noted. "Like what we saw at the hog ranch. Missouri type."

"Another Moline wagon," Ayers said, slapping the wagon's sideboards.

Together, they climbed into the rear of the wagon, likewise shuttered by canvas.

The moment they pulled back the cover, Jesse got the unwelcome smell. Not a stench, but the musty smell of old, damp, much-used clothing, and piles of old shoes and boots, and stacked clothing. They found men's coats and vests, suspenders and belts. Some men's hats, no sombreros, hats such as farmers would wear, flat crowns with wide brims. And women's garments.

Picking up a long, calico dress, Ayers muttered, "Look at this. You wonder how—" and cut himself short.

Jesse didn't speak. It was as if each didn't want to put into words what was really on their minds.

Digging farther, they found babies' clothes and little shoes, and rag dolls, their tiny, smudged faces smiling up at them.

A vague and troubling unease Jesse didn't want to admit was taking shape within him. He stopped suddenly, staring at the breast of a man's coat. "Look at this—there's blood on it."

Ayers looked, but said nothing. In silence, they explored faster, looking for what they didn't exactly know, but attracted by a mounting dread of something strange and grisly that awaited them.

A wooden box contained men's watches, some on chains with fraternal emblems, brooches and women's combs, some pretty necklaces of green and amber, some tintypes, these faces seeming forlornly sad and forgotten, lost in the millrace of time.

A small, upright metal music box startled them when Ayers picked it up and it played "Little Brown Jug." In a still smaller box within the wooden one, they found handfuls of rings, men's and women's. Jesse picked up a plain gold wedding ring and laid it in the palm of his left hand, and across his mind's eye flashed the golden-haired young woman and the little boy, who had no need to die.

Ayers looked at it and solemnly shook his head. Lips compressed, Jesse carefully put the ring back and closed the box.

As if they could not delay, as if they had to see everything here, they worked faster toward the head of the wagon. They moved coal-oil lanterns, buckets, blackened coffeepots, boxes of dishes packed with grass, a variety of tools—hammers, sledges, wedges, picks, saws, a garden rake, several small tables and a low, slim-backed rocking chair of the type which Jesse remembered his maternal grandmother calling a slipper rocker, and in which no other person dared sit.

The singular strangeness was growing increasingly heavier upon them when they uncovered a trunk, reinforced with metal strips over its oval top. Jesse opened it, surprised at its near emptiness. A bloody shirt. Under it a folded broadcloth coat such as a man might wear on Sunday. Under it some scattered papers and a Farmer's Manual. Some bills of sale. One for a team of "sound, four-year-old mules," dated March 2, 1867. Another for a "saddle horse of regis-tered Kentucky blood."

Jesse showed them to Ayers. There were more bills of sale, but he put them aside while the lieutenant rummaged deeper. Ayers held up a newspaper taken from the trunk's bottom and unfolded it so both could see the first page. It was a copy of the *Fort Smith Ga-zette*. Down the right-hand column Jesse read a headline about farm families leaving for California. Pieces of the following story leaped out at him: "Hard times in Arkansas . . . better prospects on the West Coast. . . . A paradise on earth, one returning farmer said. . . . Another Garden of Eden . . . the beautiful sea . . . a land of perpetual sunshine."

The story went on, but they had read enough. Their eyes locked. Ayers swallowed hard, and Jesse heard his own thoughts echoed as Ayers said, "Everything ties in, doesn't it? From the big mules to the Moline wagons—now this. Some of the loot came from the

Benedict train. The rest is an accumulation from other trains, bound for the market at Janos."

"Ramos?" Jesse ventured in a skeptical tone.

"But where were the Apaches?"

"Doesn't fit at all, does it?"

"Then who and why?"

Nine

They bivouacked that evening by a sweet-water spring in the Floridas, the obliging Mexican teamsters driving two of the wagons. The weary detail watered and fed, put the mounts on picket line, tied the mules to the wagons, provided what little comfort possible for the wounded and quickly made supper fires.

"You led us right to the spring," Jesse said approvingly to Ayers. "Pays to know the country."

"Now that you know where it is, you've added to your scout's knowledge. On top of that, you speak passable Spanish. I savvy it a bit, but I don't speak half as well as you do."

"You never give up, do you, Tom?"

"I still say a man should get paid if he does the work. You were one of us today. That will go into my report. The Old Man will want every detail, as you know."

Jesse let it drop.

The meager field rations brought ease. Afterward, Jesse and Ayers crossed to the Mexicans. Deciding it best to keep the prisoners separated for interrogation purposes, Ayers had ordered the white man held out of earshot of the friendly teamsters.

"Do you both farm on the Mimbres?" Jesse asked in Spanish.

"Yes, *señor,*" one replied.

"Who hired you to drive the wagons?"

"A Mexican. He promised many pesos, and we are poor."

"Who was this Mexican?"

The prisoner hesitated. "We do not know this man."

"All we want is the truth," Jesse said. "You've already involved yourself with these smugglers and murderers. If you don't tell the truth, you'll be sent to prison for many years by the U.S. Army." He was lying, but he was trying to scare the man into truth. "Now, who was this man? Was he the man called Ramos? The Ramos who raids wagon trains on the Butterfield Trail and murders immigrants for their goods and teams, teams you drove today and goods you carried."

The prisoner, older of the two, thin and somewhat stooped, looked back at Jesse through frightened eyes. *"Señor,* I swear by all the saints that we did not know this man. Never see him before."

"Did you ever hear of Ramos?"

"Yes, many times."

"Did you ever see him?"

"If I saw him, I did not know it."

"Where did you hear about him?"

"When neighbors talk." He waved a work-roughened hand. "When there is tequila and sometimes men speak in whispers about things they heard in the mountains."

"What do you hear this Ramos looks like?"

"Sometimes like Mexican, sometimes like Apache. Dress like *caballero* on prancing horse. Big sombrero. Silver buttons on vest. Very thin man. Very tall. Very big mustache like bird wings." He smiled as he said the last, and drew both forefingers across his face in exaggeration. "Then no mustache. Is Apache. Buckskin shirt. Leggings. Headband."

Ayers said, "Ask him if he knows where Ramos's camp is."

When Jesse asked, the Mexican gave a sudden rejecting jerk of his head. "No, *señor.* And nobody I know has been there."

"If you don't know where the camp is, how did you know where to meet the wagons?"

"They come for us on horseback."

"And where did they take you?"

"Below the mountains."

"Any particular place?"

"Above Fort Cummings near the mountains."

"You were hired to drive the wagons to Janos?"

"Yes, *señor.*"

"There is a store and saloon not far from the fort. The wagons stopped there last night. Why?"

"We changed mules for one wagon."

"Why just one wagon?"

"I was told they needed fresh mules for only one wagon."

"Who was in charge of the wagons?"

He shrugged. "They told us Mexicans nothing. All we could think of was the money. We were fools to go."

"You're alive—that's the important thing," Jesse told him, feeling he'd been told the truth.

Ayers said, "Tell them we'll see that they get back to their homes, but it may take a few days."

Jesse relayed that and they approached the Anglo prisoner.

He sat hunched, hands tied behind him, showing no concern whatever. He grinned up at them and jogged his head, his manner reminding Jesse of a traveling salesman selling cheap wares to unsuspecting country folk.

"Evening, gents," he said in a wheedling voice. His grin kept spreading until it became a gap-toothed smile as yellow as corn kernels in the owlish face. When it did, Jesse felt a returning stab of recognition. But he gave no hint that he knew the man.

Ayers faced him directly, and in a formal, courteous voice said, "I am Lieutenant Ayers, Third Cavalry, posted at Fort Cummings. This is Mr. Wilder. What is your name, sir?"

Again the toothy grin. "Jones—call me Jones."

"I want your real name."

"Jones is good enough. Call me Jones."

"No first name?"

"John will do." He was trying to make it sound comical.

"Regardless of what your name is, which I don't think is Jones, you have got yourself into most serious trouble. When we reach Fort Cummings, you will go into the guardhouse, held under arrest for civilian authorities."

"Under arrest? What for?"

"Several reasons. In connection with contraband being trans-ported to the Mexican border and in connection with the murder of immigrants on the Butterfield Trail, and the looting of their wagon trains, and firing at U.S. cavalry."

The man's guile dropped a notch. "I don't know nothin' about no immigrants bein' murdered an' wagons looted." Mouth open, he looked up at them with all the aplomb of a confidence artist.

"You must know a great deal, since you were an armed guard on one of the loot wagons."

"That's it—that's all I was, a hired guard. An' I didn't shoot at any of you boys in the good ol' blue. No, sirree. You didn't see me fire no shots, didja?"

"The Mexican teamster said you made him go on."

"I did—tryin' to get away from all the shootin'. I got rattled an' I got plumb scared."

"You say you hired on as a guard. When and where were you hired?"

"Back there at that little store close to the fort. I was on the lookout for work . . . anything . . . just rode in the evening be-fore . . . when them wagons came in late. They said they needed a man, so I hired on right there. Told me they needed a guard in case bandits jumped 'em down in Chihuahua. Sure didn't ask no ques-tions, me a hungry man. Good wages, too."

"How much?"

"Fifty dollars to the border."

"You mean to Janos, where the loot was to be sold."

"They didn't say Janos. Just to the border."

Ayers, his patience taxed, yielded to Jesse, who said, "Yes, I want to talk to *Mr. Jones.*" He grabbed the prisoner by the front of his shirt and heaved him to his feet. "You," he said, "are the sidekick of Gat Shell," and let that register.

The man blinked, gulped. He started to deny it, but Jesse shook him hard and said, "Don't you try to wiggle out of that. At Mesilla, Gat Shell tried to steal my horse tied in front of the saloon. I caught him in the act, just after my horse threw him. I threatened to shoot him. Made a mistake when I didn't. He wanted to carry the matter further. You calmed him down and took him away. Your partner

Gat Shell, he called you by name—called you Clinch. What do you say to that?"

Clinch's eyes bugged. Some of his cockiness faded, replaced by a fawning. "Yeah, Gat Shell used to call me Clinch." As if that finished it and didn't matter.

Jesse plopped him down hard on his haunches. "What do you mean, *used to*? You two rode with the Benedict wagon train out of Mesilla. You two were still with the train when it left Slocum's Ranch, when that god-damned fool Benedict decided to break away from the escort so he could make faster time." He waited for that to take effect, but Clinch's expression didn't alter in the slightest. The man was unshakable. "Benedict's train was wiped out," Jesse went on. "We found all the bodies but yours and Shell's. Kinda odd, wouldn't you say, since you two left with the train? Can you explain that?"

"Wiped out? Godamighty!" Clinch blurted out the words and shuttered his eyes and looked down, shaking his head. "All them poor women folks an' them poor little kids." He sniffed and fell silent, apparently overcome. If he wasn't sincere, Jesse thought, he was putting on a convincing act.

"Answer the question," Jesse kept after him. "What happened to you and Shell? Why didn't you go down with the train? You'd better have a good excuse."

Some seconds passed before Clinch cleared his throat and looked up, his facile face even more eager to please, still exhibiting the loathsome yellow grin. "Just lucky, I reckon," he said. "See, Gat an' me, well . . . him an' me split up after the train left Goodsight Station. Gat owed me money, though I knowed he had it on 'im. He's like that—got that mean streak in 'im, as much as I've helped that boy ever since we left Texas . . . kept 'im out of trouble. Shows you the thanks a man gets sometimes. We's both brought up around Sherman, Texas. His daddy an' mine—"

"Cut out the palaver," Jesse told him. "What happened after Goodsight?"

"I's just comin' to that, yes, sirree. Benedict was movin' the train fast with them big Missouri mules. Claimed he wanted to make the fort before dark. My horse went lame an' Gat, with that mean spell on 'im, wouldn't hold up. Said he didn't give a hoot if the 'Paches got me—just rode on with Benedict, leavin' me afoot, you might say, by the trail. That's the last I seen of Gat Shell to this day. Shows the thanks a man gets."

Jesse let time run a spell before he said, "So Shell goes on with Benedict and is not found with the rest of the slaughtered folks in the train, which strains any stretch of logic, and you, what happened to you?"

"Well, sir, I'd heard tell there was a Mexican family that lived south of the old trail a little piece, made a livin' at Slocum's off and on, when needed—I headed there." He gazed down at his feet and blubbered. "Tore me up what I found. The Mexican an' his wife a-layin' there. All hacked an' scalped. 'Paches got 'em.'"

"It's always the Apaches, isn't it?" Jesse said. "Yet Apaches don't scalp."

"I tell you them folks was scalped."

"Then what happened?" Jesse asked, looking off.

"I started leadin' my sore-footed horse to the store."

"You first said you rode in that night."

"Well, I'd ride a little while, then I'd walk a little while. That way I managed to get in."

"You sure that's all the story you can make up?"

"No make up to it. Just proves a man can sure get hisself in a helluva fix just tryin' to make an honest livin', or what looks honest, but sometimes ain't." He hung his head again, and when he looked up, he'd put on a pathetic face. "I should never have left Texas or met up with Gat Shell—that's gospel."

"That's also enough," Jesse said, finished, feeling disgust.

"Sir," Ayers said, facing Clinch, "I remind you that you are in the custody of the United States Army. When we reach Fort Cummings, the commanding officer will inform you of the disposition of your case. You may be taken to Mesilla for trial. I suggest that you start giving some thought to what you will testify to authorities. Tell the truth and you can help yourself. In addition to what Mr. Wilder has asked you, I should like to know, for my report, the identities of the men with the wagons who lost their lives today."

"I didn't get to see all of 'em, and the ones I did see didn't tell me their names, an' they didn't ask me mine."

"Who hired you?"

"A white man. Like I said, no name."

"There were two Indians. What was their tribe?"

"We never spoke. All I know is they dressed like white men, seemed proud of it. They kept to themselves."

"Two riders got away. Who were they?"

"One of 'em was the man that hired me—that's all I can tell you. Like I said, I didn't know ary man in the whole outfit."

Ayers was about to walk away when Jesse said, "Wait . . . Clinch, you said you rode up to the store in the evening, and when the wagons came in later, you got hired. You had to talk to Jacob Vane, who runs the store and saloon and hires the prostitutes. You did talk to him, didn't you?"

"I talked to a white man."

"Did he tell you that wagons would be coming in sometime that night and they might need a man?"

Clinch didn't bat an eye. "Nope. He didn't tell me nothin', an' he didn't tell me his name was Vane."

Jesse stepped back, knowing any further questions were useless. As he and Ayers walked off, Jesse said, "I don't believe a word the slippery little bastard said. But if he'd let drop that Vane knew the wagons were coming, we'd have Vane linked to this whole murderous operation."

"The deeper we dig into this," Ayers said wearily, "the bigger it gets. Like uncovering a bottomless cesspool."

The fires died down and the camp sounds fell away to the murmurings of tired troopers, others already snoring, and now and then the crunch of a sentry's boot on gravel and a horse or mule stirring. The red horse, ever a busy keeper, was hustling for scarce grass in the flinty soil.

In his blankets, Jesse looked back at the day. Young Ayers had handled himself quite well, demonstrating leadership and decisive action without vacillating, and showing consideration for his men. In turn, they respected him, looked to him. With good luck and opportunity, he'd make colonel before he retired. After thirty years' service, a man needed both good luck and favorable chances, pitted against the appallingly slow rate of promotion in the Yankees' postwar army. . . . He could see fingers of lightning flickering across the border sky. The tricky rainy season, playing hide-and-seek of late, was building up again—maybe, maybe not. Tonight the cool air felt heavier on the wings of a light wind whimpering through the bivouac.

For a brief spell, he let his thoughts return to Mexico. It was like an addictive weakness, a relapse into the wasting self-pity he detested. But the prisoner kept thrusting into his mind. More what Clinch hadn't said than the little he had said. A tough-minded man. An accomplished liar. . . . Well, some time in the guardhouse might improve his memory, plus the unwelcome prospects of facing civilian prosecution. There was enough evidence in the wagons to hang a dozen men. The only trouble was linking it to individuals. Yet, Clinch and Shell were the last white men seen with the Benedict train before the ambush. Plenty of witnesses could testify to that.

He slept on that line of hopeful jurisprudence, drifting into deep sleep as tired muscles relaxed in the warmth of heavy blankets. In his ears the rustling movements of his horse.

A crash shook him awake, the sound of a horse running over the rocky footing, away from the bivouac. Reaching for the Spencer, he sprang to his feet. Shafts of gray light were breaking up the night.

A carbine banged.

The horse kept going, the hoofbeats already fading to the north.

He heard Ayers calling for O'Grady. The two ran up at the same time.

"Sor," O'Grady said, his voice dismal, "it's the prisoner. He got one of the horses that was tied to the far wagon. Didn't put 'em on picket line. Afraid they wouldn't get along with our mounts."

"I understand that, but how the hell?"

"Sor, since his hands was tied behind him, we didn't search him for a knife. He must've cut himself free."

"No other way," Ayers agreed. "I failed to order him searched. Never thought of it. He seemed like such a meek prisoner."

Jesse could almost read the lieutenant's other thoughts at that moment. *What would the Old Man say to a prisoner escaping? A good deal!*

"I should've thought of it, meself, sor," O'Grady said.

"Never mind. I think we might as well fix breakfast now, Sergeant. I want to make the post with daylight to spare."

Ten

Supplies from Tucson, by way of a little-known Indian trail through the Burro Mountains west of the Mimbres River and free of Apache attacks, had arrived that morning by pack train. Among other essentials and luxuries, they contained his favorite Spanish sherry, with which he was now indulging himself. He had never understood how Americans could throw down the swill they called whiskey; however, one should not expect better of the loud-mouthed, unrefined civilian element found on the boisterous Southwestern frontier, often illiterate and physically dirty, unaware of the finer sensibilities of life and with no desire to learn. Among them, and no better, the uncouth Irish troopers of the United States Cavalry, lowly Micks laboring for thirteen dollars a month and rations a hungry dog might find unpalatable at times.

He had another white California grape, savoring its essence all the more after being brought so far in baskets. Few people of such astute discrimination, if any, he reflected, existed besides himself in this crude land. Sipping again, he considered with satisfaction the safe supply route through the rugged Burros, thanks to Ramos. There were ways to keep agreements with the Apaches, and also ways to make them *appear* to have been kept. Such as presenting a few old rifles and carbines, done with ceremony and occasional "good will" jugs of mescal, which Apaches particularly prized, drinking when received until all was gone, usually obtained only when raiding into Chihuahua and Sonora. Apaches doted on ceremony. He smiled, considering how easily some people could be led through superior thinking. The European mind vs. the primitive.

For a time he had feared that detachments from the new American Army post of Fort Bayard, northwest of his stronghold in the Mimbres Mountains, might stumble onto the trail and intercept a pack train and ask questions. But the plodding Americans had enough problems in the vicinity of the post, chasing Apache horse thieves and war parties—Apaches they never seemed to catch—without ranging far away to encounter matters that would only puzzle the Eastern-trained minds of officers preferring the comforts of post life. The same could be said for Fort Cummings and its motley garrison, whose main mission seemed to be escorting trains of fool immigrants, while about them moved events beyond their limited comprehension. More fools!

He finished the bottle, opened another and poured a long-stemmed glass three-quarters full. One never filled a wineglass to the brim. An uncouth American would have run it over. For a full ten seconds he held the glass up to the dazzling morning light, admiring its amber tint. Another sip and he stepped before a long, oval-shaped mirror framed in mahogany to regard himself, *El Comandante,* staggering a little as he did. He held a special appreciation for the mirror; once it had graced a fine Mexican home in El Paso and had been destined for a home in Tucson. He made a pompous little bow. One might say, fine things to those of cultivated taste.

Regarding himself while he rubbed the D-shaped scar above each jaw, he saw a face that was stern and austere, even priestly. His blond hair was thin and combed straight back. His prideful beard clipped close, his mouth firm and thin and flat. The eyes were his dominant feature: icy blue and piercing, in them a staring quality that could make a man look away and a pretty young woman feel instant unease, as if the eyes stripped her of every stitch of clothing.

He stood ramrod straight, a military figure honed from his days as a German uhlan: square, muscular shoulders on a stout body of surprising strength and agility, now attired in impeccable buckskins, the trouser legs stuffed into black boots. Perhaps, he admitted now, he had made a mistake when he murdered the paymaster for the regiment's funds and fled to France, then Holland, then to England. He might have worked his way up through the ranks to a commission in the Fatherland. He had the mind and the instincts for it, including a necessary indifference for loss of life around him. The objective was the thing, to be taken at all costs. A leader could not afford to let minor distractions deter him from his battle plan. For a while he had enjoyed all the fruits of high living offered in London. When the paymaster's funds ran out, he had taken stock of his prospects and, forced by circumstances, joined the British Army, which he soon despised and felt beneath him. The British had no imagination, using some of the same blundering tactics that had cost them their colonies in America. Furthermore, the officers were stodgy and aloof, bound to archaic concepts of warfare. He soon recognized that his own obvious abilities were not only being ignored, but also put down and himself relegated to the guardhouse when he raised his voice to this or that.

He began to think of Spain. Besides his bent for things military, he had a quick mind for languages, among them Spanish. He was ready to desert when, to his shock, his regiment was ordered to Canada, which was like the end of the world. Within weeks he had deserted, taking with him enough commissary funds to last for a long spree in Philadelphia, in his wake a murdered clerk. Once again, faced with depleted resources, he turned to his old standby, the military, this time the Third United States Cavalry. The Civil War was over and there were no citizenship requirements for enlistment. Therefore, he swore "to bear true faith and allegiance to the United States of America . . . to serve them honestly and faithfully against all their enemies." But he liked the Americans and the strong representation of Irish no better than he had the stuffy British, though his experience at close-order drill as a foot soldier was soon noticed, and by the time the regiment was posted at Fort Cummings, he was Corporal Karl Fogel, shortly busted to private, and after a while up to acting corporal. He kept getting into fights with the Irish, who wouldn't suffer his dictatorial manner and haughty self-importance. When he learned where the post trader kept his cash, he made plans.

The stupid Americans didn't know about Jacob Vane and what went on at his place, a magnet for drifters and malcontents, thieves and cutthroats of many breeds. Through Vane, at a goodly price, he had a saddled horse waiting in the mesquites the night he deserted with the money, some several thousand dollars, enough to last for months, if he didn't give in to his failing for drink and a retinue of easy women. His plan was to make El Paso, from there slip across the border to Paso del Norte, then Chihuahua City or Mexico City, depending on his mood. His knowledge of the language, including French, combined with his military bearing and grasp of drill and tactics, no doubt would impress the naive Mexicans. Before long he would be commissioned.

But for once, the obtuse Americans outdid themselves, performing in a military manner. He was going at a steady trot on the other side of Goodsight Station, envisioning the pleasures awaiting him, when a detail suddenly charged up and caught him. He had misjudged them, figuring they'd not even pursue, let alone be able to read his tracks on the well-traveled trail. He could still hear the despised Sergeant O'Grady's exulting voice, "Now, Fogel, where did ye think a man would desert to out here? Over fifty miles to the border, Janos miles south of that? Go west to Tucson, through desert and mountains infested with thim red devils? Why, to Mesilla and El Paso—where else, where the beer is cool and no man's a stranger to the girls, even an ugly Dutchy like you. Besides, yer tracks was the only fresh ones on the trail. Like readin' a child's picture book, so simple it was. . . . Tie him across the saddle, boys. We want to take him back in the proper style to which he is unaccustomed."

Fogel was desperate. "I'll split what I took if you'll let me ride on."

"Then we'd be just as faithless as you. May the saints forbid. Tie 'im up, boys."

"You'll pay for this someday," Fogel swore at them. "Every man!"

"Someday we'll all pay up, Dutchy, but ye won't be the one a-dishin' it out—that's for certain."

The pain and humiliation that followed was nearly more than he could endure. A Mexican muleteer delivered the fifty lashes, and a cavalry farrier branded a *D* on each cheek. But his remarkably tough body and iron will got him through; all during his ordeal, he kept thinking of revenge and how he would go about getting it. Especially on Colonel Taylor, who had ordered the punishment and stood by watching while it was applied.

He rubbed the scars again. The day would come, and soon, if he could only arrive at a surefire plan, each step carefully plotted. The opportunity would come if he was patient. Sometimes the thirty-some cutthroats in his gang, which he liked to think of as his command, most of them illiterates, had to be shown each little move, but murder they understood thoroughly without instruction. In return, he furnished them a refuge here in the Mimbres Mountains. Plenty of food, some drink, though he had learned to be careful about dispensing liquor, generally making it available in quantity only when they returned from a successful objective. Sometimes, however, they brought in their own from the mining camps, and then there were disciplinary problems. A few degenerate women helped ease their tension, but could also add to it. A brutal bunch to command, sometimes they even offended him. Several were U.S. Army deserters from the East who had killed to avoid being captured; others were wanted for murder by civilian authorities in the states. Some were on the Texas Rangers' wanted list, and for that reason would never go back. Mostly white men in camp. A few American Indians, who hated whites, and had reason to, they said. A few blacks, all former slaves, who did the cooking and camp chores. All had murdered whites, one an overseer, one a white whore in New Orleans. A sprinkling of Mexicans, former bandits, who hated gringos and had no qualms about preying on their own people.

In return for their services—he hesitated to say loyalty—he expected discipline in camp and while carrying out an objective. Twice he had exacted it, gunning down both drunks in front of the others when they cursed him and made some foolishly menacing moves. Both were American outlaws, which gave him a rather secret pleasure, because he hated the stupid Americans most of all. Other times, when a man announced that he was quitting the command—

who knew what he might do out of spite, even leading a cavalry detachment to the stronghold?—Fogel had him followed and killed. No less a simple matter of self-preservation one must follow.

It was Ramos, his second in command, who carried out such quests of vital importance to the entire command's safety. Ramos, born a Mexican in Chihuahua, stolen and reared as a Warm Springs Apache to hate all White Eyes, as he called the American invaders of his homeland, and who thought no more of killing a White Eye, man, woman or child, than he would squashing an ant under his moccasined foot. Likewise for Mexican travelers on the trail, because Apaches hated Mexicans. An extraordinarily intelligent man, Ramos had learned English hanging around army posts on the Rio Grande; that way he could pretend to be a friendly Indian or an educated Mexican, and dress as such, whichever role suited his purpose.

Fogel had wanted to ambush a Fort Cummings wood-cutting detail in the mountains, but the cautious Americans always posted guards all around. He'd planned and worked out a maneuver to wipe out an escort detail, but the Americans always put out flankers, and the open country between Mesilla and the fort was opportune only for ambush when stalking unwary wagon trains with foolhardy leaders, green to the Southwest, like the braggart who had led the Benedict train to its destruction.

From lookout posts in the foothills overlooking the fort, he had scouts with field glasses scanning the post and environs daily. An attack on the walled fort was out of the question. *El Comandante is not that foolish, sir.* He saw himself as a military officer of high rank, born to command divisions and corps instead of a band of thugs, and would be doing so today if fate had dealt him a fair hand and he'd come from Prussian nobility instead of being the son of a shoe cobbler. He searched for the proper words to describe his ignored military genius. . . . *Leader and strategist*—that was it. There his true talents lay. He swelled at the thought and rubbed his scarred face again, feeling his rage for revenge rise with the touch. *The time will come, Colonel Taylor. I assure you it will come, sir. It will because El Comandante so orders.*

He had another sip of wine, and his thoughts spun back to *that day.* Staggering and cursing like a wild man through the post's gates to the tune of the "Rogue's March," he had made his way to Jacob Vane's. Vane had shown little sympathy, but ordered a prostitute to treat his face and lacerated back with warm soapy water and to bandage him.

Next day Vane said, "You were a fool to do it the way you did. Instead of running, why didn't you leave the money with me and go back to the fort and desert later?"

"Leave the money with you?"

"Birds of a feather flock together, my friend. My way nobody would have connected you to the money. I made a mistake when I let you have the horse. I should've known what was up your sleeve, but I thought desertion was all you had in mind. You should have trusted Jacob Vane, taken him into your confidence. He could have saved you all the pain—and the money. Maybe you have learned a lesson."

Fogel groaned as he moved his shoulders. "What possible lesson?"

"How to get back at the blue-bellies, get back at Colonel Taylor. And, if you're patient, make yourself rich."

"How?" At that moment Fogel's pain overrode any thought of wealth.

Over a brand of whiskey which Vane didn't serve his customers, he laid out a plan.

Many drifters gravitated to his establishment, he said, men who would do anything for food, shelter, women, whiskey and a little money—steal, murder, torture, rape. They could be organized into a working band by the right man, a man with force and intelligence.

Fogel nearly blacked out. He reached for the bottle again. Through his fog of pain, he asked, "How do you mean? What would they do?"

"Knock off unescorted immigrant trains."

"You mean . . . wipe 'em out?"

"Exactly. No survivors, no witnesses. You wouldn't want anybody to survive to tell the story. You might hang."

Fogel straightened in his chair, taken aback. "Where does the money come from?"

"You strip the wagons of everything usable and take the stock. Take what wagons you need."

Fogel said nothing. He hurt too much.

Vane leaned closer. "That's not all. You strip the bodies of clothing, boots, shoes, jewelry—everything."

"Sounds ghoulish."

"It is—but this is harsh country. Consider how the United States cavalry goes about killing Apaches whenever it can, even shooting into Apache camps. Sometimes killing women and children."

Fogel permitted himself a dubious but painful smile. "What would be done with the loot?"

"You haul it to Janos. There's a market there for everything people use. I have a contact there, the best. None other than the mayor —the *alcalde*. The kind of contact you need. He'd choke his grandmother for a peso or a string of red chilis. Everything works through him. He pays you and what he doesn't sell around the local plaza and outlying ranches is hauled farther into Mexico, where there are other markets as good."

"I still don't see it."

"There's an endless market in Mexico for all goods. Mexico, itself, produces very little. A market that's waiting to be tapped. And don't forget the demand for horses and mules, and guns of any make or caliber for fighting Apaches. Also, a good wagon brings good money—as high as five hundred pesos."

"If the market's so good, why haven't you tapped it?"

"I've peddled some goods picked up here in trade. That's how I found out about it. But on a large scale it will take a man of military experience, an organizer—a man of force who can hold a bunch of cutthroats together. A man to rule them with an iron hand. I could market the stuff, but I'm not a military man like you."

Fogel's head was throbbing and his lashed back was almost more than he could stand. He wobbled to his feet. "Better look for another man. Right now I need a bed."

He was surprised when Vane led him to a room with a decent bed in the rear of the adobe. He passed out the moment he eased down and stretched out on his side.

It was evening when he woke up, aroused by his wracking pain. There was a woman in the room. Not the heavy-bodied, pulpy-faced Anglo woman of lost years who had treated his wounds. This one also was white, but she was much younger and slender, with a tough, inscrutable, leathery face that could have been somewhat pretty under genteel circumstances. He saw that in the lamplight. A better quality than what Vane usually brought in, he thought.

"Time to eat," she said, and left the room. She returned with a bowl of soup and some bread.

"I need whiskey first," he told her.

She shrugged and left again, returned holding a bottle and glass, into which she poured a stiff drink. Groaning, he sat up and clutched the glass, threw down the drink and instantly spluttered, his throat on fire.

"What the hell?" he gagged. "It's rotgut. I meant good whiskey."

"It's all I could find," she said matter-of-factly. "Vane hides the good stuff. Now you eat." She left the room.

He finished the soup and bread and lay on his side. The food and whiskey had helped him relax. He fell into an on-and-off sleep, slivers of pain shooting through his back and across his jaws like knives. But he did sleep.

Much later, he became aware of a woman's slim, naked body beside him and a hand sliding inside his trousers. He felt an instant response. She laughed. Her hand stopped, then squeezed him.

"Let's take off them pants," she said, rising.

He recognized her flat voice. "Don't think I'm up to anything, the way I hurt."

"You will be. You'll see. You'll feel better."

He unbuckled his belt and she pulled off his trousers and lay beside him, reaching for him.

"Watch my back."

"I won't touch your back. Won't have to." She snuggled in closer, sliding under him a little, lifting her left hip, her left leg over his thigh, stroking and guiding him. She smelled of some cheap lilac scent. Her breath came hot and fast on his face. She tightened on him and he forgot his pain.

After a while, she said, "You're good—real good. You're better than the soldier boys. They either get too drunk and I have to do all the work, or they get in too big a hurry."

When it was over, she left him and after a short time came back with a lamp and washed and dried him and helped him on with his trousers.

"Better sleep some more," she said in that voice. "Vane wants to talk to you in the morning."

"I hurt too much to sleep."

"You will. Just be still. You'll see."

"What's your name? Believe you're new here."

"What's in a name anyway?" she replied. Then she walked to the doorway and paused, seemingly amused, holding the lamp, its rays showing the taut lines of her impassive face. "Just call me the New One, if you think I have to have a name."

He dropped off into a deep sleep.

Pain broke his sleep. He flinched at the mere touch of his back. His face was horribly swollen. He had fever. It was already daylight. He smelled coffee and heard the approaching rattle of dishes. A shy Mexican girl brought his breakfast of black coffee, biscuits and greasy bacon and helped him sit up. He ate with gusto.

Finished, he lay on his side, thinking, going over what Vane had broached. It didn't appeal to him; nothing did this morning. He would hurt for days and he would carry the *D* scars on his face for life, though careful trimming of his beard would help cover his shame. He was a vain man and the scars worried him much more than his flayed back.

Lying there, hurting, scarred for life, he could think only of Colonel Taylor and his troopers. They'd seemed to relish his punishment, because they'd never liked him, because they'd said to his face that he was overbearing and arrogant. His mind drew him back to every detail of his ordeal: each lash of the whip as his body gave in to the pain, while he refused to cry out; the branding, first on his left cheek, the sickening smell of his own burned flesh, then the right cheek and the stink of more burned flesh. All the while, the martinet Taylor standing there, arms folded, like some mighty conqueror, not missing a thing. Taylor signaling the drummer to commence the roll drumming him out of the post. Furthermore, he'd been left afoot, not even a mule to ride, only a canteen to get him through. A virtual death sentence on the desert in his weakened condition had it not been for Jacob Vane. Yet Vane, he reminded himself, wouldn't have taken him in unless he'd seen some way to use a dishonorably discharged soldier for his own gain.

He touched his left cheek again, his newly acquired gesture that would remain with him as a reminder until he could exact revenge upon Taylor. But revenge would take time, and he would have to curb his impatience, learn to wait until the right opportunity presented itself. Jacob Vane offered him the one chance he had, at least the beginning of it.

He found Vane waiting for him in an office off the long bar. Sometimes Vane with his corpulent mass reminded him of a giant toad. Vane looked him up and down. "You look like hell," he said, "but I can see you're in a better frame of mind than yesterday." A knowing half-grin. "Roxie can improve a man's outlook. I might even let you take her along when you get established, though you might find it taxing to keep her from getting restless."

"I've never failed to satisfy a woman."

"Every man has his limits, my friend. And age is one of them." His expression was worldly-wise. "What I'm getting around to is . . . you will survive all you've been through and your revenge will come in due time . . . along with the riches . . . if you're patient and if you listen to Jacob Vane. You want revenge, don't you?"

"You know I do. How else would a man think, if he's a man at all —particularly a military man like me, a man with my experience and training?"

Nodding, Vane poured Fogel a drink of whiskey.

It was not, Fogel discovered, warily sipping, what Roxie had brought him last night. He tossed it down. "What else do you have to tell me?"

"Like I said, I can get the men you need, but it will require a little time. I have five here now on the dodge. All coldblooded killers. Others will be drifting in if you say so. I can send a man to El Paso today to pass the word to rendezvous here. News will get around and spread into Texas, the mother lode of outlaws."

"A sort of call to arms, eh?" Fogel said. The good whiskey warmed his belly and his outlook. He had another slug.

"I'm known all over the Southwest, as far as Indian Territory," Vane reminded him. "I keep my word. A wanted man comes to me, I help him a little. Not too much—that would be a mistake. He might try to kill me for what I have. First, I give him a place to lay over and hide, with food, clothing, a few drinks and a woman. In turn, he owes me. . . . You'd be surprised at what they bring me—guns, jewelry, gold nuggets, sometimes diamonds. I give them a little on it. Later, I fence it in El Paso or El Paso del Norte for a nice piece of money. I also have a market contact in New Orleans."

"How many men do you think this will take?"

"Thirty or so. You don't want a big bunch. Could create trouble. Somebody might want to take over the operation from you. Keep the outfit tight and under control. Keep in mind that some men will drift on. Some won't go for it, tough as they are. There will be losses, but not many, if you plan the ambushes right. You're a military man, as you say. You'd have to determine that."

Some doubts broke through Fogel's whiskey fog. "Where do I get the guns?"

"From Jacob Vane; however, the weapons are varied, as you might expect. We may have to send to Mesilla or El Paso for more guns and adequate ammunition."

"You make it sound easy. But it won't be. How would I know what trains to hit?"

"In the first place, you would never attack a train under cavalry escort."

"Nothing I'd like better," Fogel swore.

"That could lead to disaster." Vane's irritation was evident, mixed with sarcasm. "From a distance you could use a handy device known as binoculars, you know? More efficient to have a man or two in Mesilla to size up wagons making up to take the trail. They could go along as guides or guards. These immigrants are green as grass. Half-scared fools who'll believe anything—glad to have another rifle or two for protection. How your spies get word to you, you'd have to work out."

"I guess that's possible."

"Where's your imagination, man? Certainly it's possible. Have your man drop out of the train for one excuse or another, then ride ahead. Mount 'im on a fast horse that can go a distance of ground. You could have another man posted at one of the old stage stops. Once he gets the word, he could pass it on to you to bring on the bunch and set up the ambush."

"We'd need a base, a stronghold," Fogel said, gazing around.

"Not here, you don't, this close to the fort. Jacob Vane is no fool. Use your imagination. What better place than in the mountains? From there you could see for miles, not only to watch for wagons, but you could see a man signaling for you to come on. I would also suggest that you keep a daily watch on the post, in case Taylor mounts a threat in your direction."

"Taylor—he's the one I want, and I don't intend to wait very long."

"You'll have to wait. Organization comes first, getting the right caliber of men on hand, training them, setting up your base in the mountains. You'll have to prepare quarters and corrals—maybe tents for the men awhile. Above all, you'll have to maintain enough discipline to hold your men together. I wouldn't rule with an iron hand, or they might mutiny, but enough to enforce authority."

"How can I be sure these outlaws will take discipline?"

"Because I know the killer type. Because I've dealt with 'em for years. Because they have no place to go. Most are in hiding now, afraid to move around much because the Rangers are on the look-out for 'em and will shoot on sight. Out here they can live a better life. Food, shelter, whiskey, women. Beats being holed up all the time."

Fogel had another drink. All he could think of was Taylor and what he would do to him. "How am I gonna get Taylor, once we get organized?"

Vane slapped the table hard. "Hell, man, ain't you the military genius, the planner? A soldier who's deserted from three armies? Where's your imagination, I ask you again? Maybe you can lure Taylor into the mountains. Fight 'im like an Apache. Ambush 'im in the mountains. I'd sure lay off a fight out in the open." He sat back and threw up a pudgy, dismissive hand and sneered. "Maybe this is all too much for you—more than you can handle?"

Fogel felt his face go hot. "I didn't say that. But I'm not too sold on attacking wagon trains on an open trail—dangerous."

"Not if you plan it right and we gather the right men to do it. Let me tell you something. There's all kinds of killers. There's nobody tougher or meaner than a Mexcan *bandido*. There'll be some Mexican bandits in the bunch, wanted by both the *federales* and the

Rangers. Besides Texas, there'll be killers outa the deep South and from back East. Maybe a few Indians. A killer's a killer. Now listen to this. Who'll everybody think is ambushin' the trains? Apaches, of course. Apaches have killed hundreds of whites and Mexicans in Arizona and New Mexico. Nobody'll think it's an organized band of mostly white cutthroats. In fact, Apaches might beat you to an unescorted train or two."

"I'd have to command with a firm hand," Fogel said. "I'd need men to help me enforce discipline."

Vane's expression was reassuring. "I expect a man to come in tomorrow who'll be all you need—just one man—Juan Ramos. You'll savvy why damn quick when you talk to him. Now, what do you say? Do you want to do it this way or not? It's the only way I see that you can get Taylor."

"After I see Ramos and talk to him. Not before. And I have a question for you before I agree. What's in this for Jacob Vane? Why are you doing this?"

Vane played a lazy smile back at him. "We're partners, and don't partners share equally? Jacob Vane, who is also a businessman with many expenses, will get half of what the loot fetches in Janos."

"Half?" Fogel protested. "I do the planning and fighting, taking all the chances, and you get half? I won't agree."

"Jacob Vane collects the men, furnishes the guns and ammunition—makes this possible. You have no other choice, friend Fogel. Jacob Vane gets half or there is no deal."

"Not till I see Ramos," Fogel said, rising, and walked out.

Half, he thought, was too much. Yet, on reflection, he realized that only through Vane's assistance could he ever get at Taylor. Without Vane, he had nothing, not even a horse or carbine or money. Jacob Vane had him, at Jacob Vane's price.

He rested during the afternoon, his waking moments alternating between the challenge of what Vane had proposed and his numbing pain and the cause of that pain, his face scarred forever. Time. Right now he needed time for his body to mend. He would have to be patient, he thought, slipping into sleep. Maybe, by holding off, he could make a better deal with Vane. . . . Once, the sound of a horse pounding off east on the trail broke his sleep. Was Vane so certain of him that he was already sending a rider to El Paso to pass the call for men?

The Mexican girl brought him a supper of black coffee, tortillas and beans. He ate with hunger. Now and then he caught the hum of voices, men and women, but the place seemed quiet; everybody was waiting, he thought, like himself.

Darkness was near when Roxie came, behind her enigmatic face an anticipation that burned like coals in her intense dark eyes. She showed him a bottle and glasses. "Some of Vane's good stuff. I found out where he hides it." She poured them both strong drinks and handed Fogel his.

He sipped while he considered her. Tough, lean, hard, driven by unquenchable need. She threw down her drink with a single swallow. "You're slow," she said. "Don't you like it?"

"I like to savor good whiskey, like good wine."

When he had finished his drink, she took his glass and put it on a stand. "Now," she said, "let's see about them pants."

"You're in a big hurry," he chided her. "I'd like another drink. Good whiskey's hard to get out here."

She poured him another and impatiently watched him finish it, sip by sip. "Men like you don't come along very often," she said, taking his glass.

"Watch my back," he said.

She helped him off with his trousers. When she pulled her dress over her head, he saw that she wore no underclothes. For a space she stood there for him to admire her proud, slim body. Then she was beside him, reaching for him.

"Remember, every man has his limits," he joked. "Jacob Vane told me that."

"That old fart," she said, laughing. "Let him speak for himself."

It was midmorning before Fogel got up and ate breakfast. Roxie had stayed well into the night, coupling with him two more times and drinking Vane's good whiskey. She was, he judged, the most insatiable woman of the many he'd satisfied, including the fancy French and English whores.

A Mexican dressed in a buckskin shirt and a red bandanna headband sat across from Vane when Fogel entered the saloon. Coal-black hair hung to the Mexican's shoulders.

Vane waved him to a chair. "Time you two met. Fogel . . . Juan Ramos."

Ramos stood and extended a firm hand, his glittery black eyes lancing over Fogel, openly measuring him. *"Señor,* it is beeg pleasure to meet you. *Señor* Vane, long my good friend, has told me of your troubles with the White Eyes at the fort, placed in my country against the wishes of my people, the Warm Springs Apaches." Although his voice was like a purr, it carried a hint of menace even here.

Ramos was tall for a Mexican. Not tall and big, but tall and thin, like a rapier, Fogel thought. Below his buckskin shirt he wore breechcloth and leather leggings. His face could have been carved from rock, so sharp were his features: the long, pronged nose, the pointed chin, the jutting cheekbones. The cutting eyes held Fogel's attention, bold and cruel. Now Fogel's eyes met those of Ramos and both stares became fixed, unwavering, until both men smiled and glanced away and back, the clash broken.

Not only cruel, but savagely cruel and sadistic, Fogel thought. *He'll do.*

Vane poured Fogel a drink and another for Ramos. Sitting down, Fogel sipped. It was the good stuff, which signified the importance of the meeting.

"Now that you've sized each other up, what do you think?" Vane asked.

After a pause, Ramos spoke first. "I can see he is strong man. I like thees man. Because he has suffered at the hands of the White Eyes, he will not hold back the knife when a White Eye, on his knees, praying like a weakling priest, whines and begs for life. Yes, *Señor* Vane, my good friend, I like thees man. We can work together. We will do many things together. We will kill many White Eyes, my new friend."

"Well?" Vane asked, looking at Fogel. "I've explained everything to Juan. He knows what will have to be done."

"Would you agree to be second in command?" Fogel said, expecting refusal, for this man was not only cruel, he was proud—killer proud.

Ramos smiled what Fogel had already learned passed for a smile, the barest parting of the thin lips over teeth as even and white as piano keys. Ramos was capable of a luxuriant mustache like many Mexicans, Fogel guessed, but instead he allowed only a tracery of black hair on his upper lip, which he probably plucked to avoid any semblance of Mexican vanity.

"*Sí, señor,* if we plan together and share the same when goods are hauled to Janos."

"We will plan together and share together like comrades," Fogel vowed, and held out his hand.

As they shook, Ramos smiled again. "To me you will be *El Co-mandante.* But do not ask me to stop killing White Eyes. They have done many wrongs to my people. As long as White Eyes are around, I will kill them. It is my pleasure."

"I hope," said Fogel, smiling broadly, "that you include many blue-bellied troopers at the fort among the White Eyes."

And smiling again in unison, they clinked glasses.

So the agreement had been reached. By now Fogel was rich by frontier standards. Time had passed, too much time, because he still had not found the opportunity to catch Colonel Taylor and kill him. Taylor seldom went anywhere without at least a platoon. An opportunity would have to be found soon, because he was feeling the call of his old, free-roving, libidinous ways. With the money he had from loot, including the gold from the Benedict train, which he had not yet actually shared with Ramos—Ramos, as intelligent as he was, naively assumed the gold, put away at headquarters, would be shared later—he could live in grand style in Mexico for several years, meanwhile impressing the Mexican government with his military credentials. Style was always important in achieving one's ends.

On that thought, he had another glass of sherry.

Eleven

A wagon broke down, causing hours of delay, and after that, Corporal Dan Casey, a son of the Old Sod, born in County Galway, Ireland, died. Therefore, the detail made a solemn dry camp for the night and pushed on in the morning, arriving around noon, parking the wagons outside the wall.

"I'd better report and get this over with," Ayers said. He made a fisted motion of frustration, his mouth grim. "One dead trooper and our lone prisoner escapes. Can't exactly say that the officer in charge acted in a commendable manner."

"Hold on," Jesse said. "The detail got what it went after—the wagons—found 'em loaded with immigrant loot. You not only cleared up what happened to the Benedict train, but to others as well, God knows."

"But I lost one man—my first. Casey was a damned good man. He and Sergeant O'Grady came to America on the same boat. Casey was like a younger brother. The Old Man will likely have services this afternoon. You can't wait too long, hot as it is."

"I know how you feel, Tom. But many times there's a price to what you have to do in war." He would not offer to go along. That would be demeaning to the young lieutenant. Jesse waited by the wagons.

Within ten minutes, Ayers and Colonel Taylor walked briskly out to the wagons. Taylor inspected each wagon in detail.

"This exceeds anything I'd expected," he said, visibly impressed. "General Wilder, Lieutenant Ayers said your Spencer carbine was quite effective, said it was a big factor in breaking up their rear guard."

"We were all concentrating our fire there, sir."

"What I wouldn't give for twenty Spencers! Despite the Ordnance Department's decision that the carbine's a tricky killer. Trained cavalrymen can handle the weapon and look out for its one eccentric quirk. You, yourself, proved that, sir. Mr. Ayers, park the wagons near the stables and dismiss the detail. You can tender your written report later. You and I and General Wilder, if he so wishes, are going calling on one Jacob Vane. Believe me, he'd better have some answers!"

As before, when they rode up to the adobe, the first face seen was that of the coarse woman Vane had called Millie. One bug-eyed glance from the doorway and she vanished.

Colonel Taylor didn't dismount. He held up a staying hand.

A wary Jacob Vane appeared moments later. "Come in for a drink, gentlemen. Don't believe I've ever had the honor of seeing so many officers at my establishment."

"Honor has nothing to do with it, Mr. Vane. I am Colonel Taylor, in command of Fort Cummings. I have news that won't please you. A detail from the post caught up with the wagons that stopped here three nights ago—wagons headed for Janos that you said were going to Mesilla. There was a hot engagement. One trooper was killed, one wounded. I believe there were seven killed in the wagons' rear guard."

Vane's reaction was a blink. "Sorry about the boys, Colonel. But what's that got to do with me?" he asked with a shrug.

"What that has to do with you, sir, is that you gave the detail deliberately misleading information as to the wagons' destination. Manifestly, that was your intention, but it didn't succeed."

"I said I thought they's headed for Mesilla. Just a guess."

"A lame excuse, when you had to have heard the wagons leaving.

I believe you also intimidated your own people here, the prostitutes, from answering when Lieutenant Ayers and Mr. Wilder asked them which way the wagons had gone. Nevertheless, we figured out where. You are on a very dangerous course here, Mr. Vane. I could close you down."

"Like hell! My place is off the military reservation. I'm a law-abiding United States citizen. You close me down, I'll raise a stink from here to Washington. I have friends. You'd see!"

"I'm sure about the stink. Whatever you do has a familiar smell to it. Whether your place is off the military reservation or not, I could arrest you for interfering with military operations designed to halt the flow of contraband into Mexico."

"What contraband?" He was, Jesse saw, playing his who-me? role of innocence.

"Everything the wagons carried, from saddles to clothing and boots and shoes to worn-out carbines. Worth thousands of dollars in Janos and on into Mexico. Some of the goods and wagons traced to the ill-fated Benedict train, recently wiped out on the trail."

"I know nothing about any contraband, as you call it. All kinds of people stop here, Colonel, and what they do after they leave here can't be blamed on me."

"Except in this case, you aided and abetted armed men taking contraband into Mexico. From this time on, you are on watchful probation."

Wheeling his mount away, with Lieutenant Ayers riding on the colonel's left as the junior officer, and Jesse on the right, Taylor said, "Nothing would be served yet by closing him down. Better to let him hang himself. By no means, I feel, have we seen the last of this."

Corporal Daly and Jaime Taylor in his sergeant's uniform were riding out of the post gate as the three riders approached. Jaime waved, shouting, "Patches is rarin' to run, General. I think he wants to go up the canyon and into the mountains."

"You know you are never to go into the canyon," his father said sternly, "or try to wander away from your escort. You are under the strictest of orders to obey Corporal Daly when out riding and to do exactly as he says. Do you understand, Sergeant?"

A chastened Jaime replied, "Yes, sir, General," and closed up beside Daly.

They rode at a slow trot for half a mile eastward on the trail. There they began a wide circle back toward the mountains, a route they usually followed, lasting about an hour, one Jaime liked better than sticking to the old trail and a boring return over it. This way he could feast his eyes on the fascinating mountains.

"Cooke's Peak must be about the biggest mountain in the whole world, Corporal Daly. What do you think?"

Daly, a good-natured Irish trooper who really liked the precocious boy, despite his sometimes vexing ways, said, "Oh, there are bigger mountains farther north in the Rockies and in other countries, but Cooke's Peak is a grand mountain, all right, Sergeant."

"Is it true you can see clear to Mexico from the peak?"

"I've never been up there, but that's what they say. Be easy."

"Wish I could see it. How far is Mexico? Two hundred miles?"

"Not that far. From here, way under a hundred."

"What countries have bigger mountains than Cooke's Peak?"

"Switzerland, for one," said Daly, whose knowledge of geography was limited to County Mayo, Ireland, from Boston westward to the Southwest, and what little he'd heard and read. "They call 'em the Swiss Alps."

"If they be bigger than Cooke's Peak, I'd like to see 'em."

"Maybe ye can when ye get to be a general. Then ye can tour Europe in grand style, takin' along yer lady fair."

"Oh, I wouldn't take a girl along."

"Just think ye wouldn't. Wait'll yer older, lad."

"I'm gonna be a general someday, like Papa was in the war. But first I'll go to West Point."

"That's a good idea. By then ye'll be so smart I won't be able to talk with yez."

"I won't forget my old friends. I'll go into the cavalry. Promotions are faster there, and when I'm general, I'll make you a major . . . no, a colonel. You're a good soldier, Corporal John Daly."

Daly smiled. The lad must be workin' up to something to call him by his first name. But it was good to hear a boy talk about his dreams. No need to shatter them. Jaime would learn soon enough how slow promotions were. "That'd be mighty generous of ye,

General Taylor, sir. I'll keep that in mind to buoy me up when I'm feelin' low and I've run out of pay. Trouble is, by the time ye want to make me colonel, I'd be too old to accept all the jumps in grade from corporal."

"I'll graduate from West Point a second lieutenant. After that, it'll just be a matter of time on my way up to brigadier."

"Yeah, time, Jaime, time."

The boy was always friendly and talkative, but more so today, such a change usually leading up to some departure from orders. They rode on awhile, not speaking, and Daly could tell that his charge was deep in thought, working on something.

"Corporal Daly, sir," Jaime said suddenly, brightly, "don't you ever get tired of riding the same old way when we go out?"

"Orders are orders, Sergeant."

"I know, the general always says that. Have you ever been up the canyon and over to the Mimbres River?"

"Many times on escort duty."

"Is the canyon on the Butterfield Trail?"

"Yeah. The trail goes through the canyon. What be ye drivin' at, lad?"

"Oh, just wondered."

"Yer doin' more than just wonderin'."

"So if you wanted to see the canyon, you'd just follow the trail past the post?" The next moment he was silent, obviously picturing how that would be in his quick, mischievous mind. "What way does it go from there?"

"Ye should know that. The trail goes past Cooke's Spring a little northwest, then swings west."

"How long is the canyon, Corporal?"

"Four or five miles."

"Just a short ride."

"A dangerous ride. Now don't ye start gettin' any such notions. I'll never take ye there."

Jaime took on an impish look, mixing in his appealing boyish smile. "Couldn't we ride in behind the fort to the spring? Couldn't you take me up the canyon just a little way, Corporal Daly, sir? Couldn't we, sir? *Just a little way?*"

"We could not, young sir. Not an inch up the trail. That'd violate me orders—orders ye know as well as me."

They weren't far from the post now. Jaime kicked the pony's fat sides and the surprised Patches leaped into a short-legged run.

Daly let him go. But after a short run, seeing that Jaime intended to take the trail past the spring, Daly spurred to a lope, calling for the boy to stop.

Instead, Jaime glanced over his shoulder, grinning prankishly, and belabored poor Patches all the harder.

Daly's patience snapped. He dashed up, going at a run, and grabbed the pony's cheekstrap and pulled him to a halt.

"Ye was headin' for trouble, lad. Not only for yerself, but meself, too. The ride is over."

"Aw, I just wanted to go up the trail to the canyon. Just a little way. *Just a little way, Corporal John Daly, sir.*"

"Not another inch. Next time I'm detailed to such aggravatin' duty, yer old friend 'Colonel Daly to be' may have a turrible belly ache and go on sick call."

After the services for Corporal Casey at the cemetery atop a hill southeast of the fort, Jesse unsaddled, turned his horse into a post corral and crossed to the bachelor officers' quarters, where he had left his gear.

He pulled off his boots and sat on a bunk, feeling his muscles loosen, feeling the tag end of his energy, letting his mind run over the rush of events these past days, and what might lie ahead for him. Should he pack up in the morning and head for Arizona, or should he stay awhile? Even take the scout's job? He'd like to answer the question of who was attacking the wagon trains, but that could take months on end or never be solved. He didn't believe the mixed party of men the detail had killed and routed made up all the people preying on the trail for plunder. It was too big an operation, too thoroughly carried out, too well planned. Others were involved. And they weren't Apaches. Not that Apaches didn't attack wagon trains.

He went on with these thoughts. Vane had a definite hand in the Janos operation, a behind-the-scenes figure in the cruelest of games for profit. Clinch was a clever little bastard, the sort of man that always seemed to land on his feet, no matter how guilty he was, and when caught, putting on that loathsome, shifty grin. And where was Gat Shell in all this? He and Clinch ran together, the little man like his shadow. Maybe Shell was one of the two who had fled.

The scene at the Benedict train was the worst brutality he'd ever come upon. Men going down in battle was brutal enough. The golden-haired young woman and the little boy were chiseled into his memory for all time. Poor unlucky innocents! Needlessly gone because one bullheaded man blind with ego had ignored common-sense warnings.

The thought of leaving troubled him, gave him a sense of incompleteness, of a lacking within himself. He lay down on the bunk to ponder the matter . . . tomorrow. The instant he closed his eyes, sleep claimed him.

Twelve

He was hitting his sherry supply again, more than usual, restless and impatient, even though it wasn't yet time for his riders and wagons to return from Janos. Ramos, a shrewd and intimidating bargainer, should report back with considerable money after delivering the goods and arms to the *alcalde*. The biggest shipment ever sent south. Fogel smiled at the prospects. Vane would get his share as usual, or would think he was getting it. There was no way he could question what he got unless he rode to Janos and asked the *alcalde*, which he would never do. The trip was too much for a fat man who was getting old.

Every day now Fogel's thoughts centered on Mexico and living as he chose, impressing public officials as an affluent international soldier of fortune, moving in high circles, speaking flawless Spanish, French and English, whatever, meeting beautiful ladies. Ah . . . He would need to create a quasi-uniform of sorts to wear in public, something austere and unassuming, yet hinting of an audacious military past. Only Colonel Taylor lay between him and his dream.

At the thought of women in Mexico, he reflected on Roxie, a gift from Jacob Vane soon after the agreement was reached. She'd been good in bed—too good, in time boring and insatiable even for lusty

Karl Fogel. He'd caught her in a tent with the lowest outlaw in the command, a madman killer from Louisiana who called himself the Wolf and boasted of thirty-eight murders. *El Comandante* could not tolerate sharing his woman. He would lose face. His band of cutthroats would sneer behind his back and might refuse to follow orders. Before long Roxie would be making the rounds with other women-starved men. Something had to be done immediately.

Ramos had handled the matter for him. No objection. Wasn't she a White Eye woman? Roxie was found in an arroyo near camp, there for all to see, naked and her throat expertly cut. Regrettable, but necessary. Above all, a military leader must protect his power of command.

The waiting and the growing delay over getting at Taylor left him frustrated and uneasy. Finishing the glass of sherry, he stepped to the door and called in a loud voice for Lucia.

She should have been nearby, waiting for him to call at any time of his choosing. But she didn't answer.

He called again.

Still no answer. Was she mocking him? Frightened and subdued at first, she'd bordered on insolent rebellion of late. He might have to look for another girl among the Mexican families on the Mimbres River. He could imagine what his men would think, lounging in idleness and playing cards, when they heard him repeating his call. The game of poker seemed to amuse stupid American outlaws more than anything, that is, next to cheap women and the swill of cheap whiskey.

He called again, bellowing her name. No reply, no Lucia. He was about to storm out there, looking for her, when she appeared at the door and entered, eyes cast down, trembling.

"Why didn't you come when I called you?"

"I was busy, *señor*."

"Busy at what?"

She seemed to force herself to look up at him, fighting her fear, her dread of what was coming and which came every day. "I have learned to sew, to fix my clothes."

"I have offered to buy you clothes, but you have refused."

"Where would I buy clothes, *señor*?"

"At the stores in Pinos Altos. I will send an escort with you."

"Ha! I am ashamed to go there. People know me . . . what I do here. I have relatives there working in the mines."

"Then you have no excuse. You won't let me buy you clothes, and soon the clothes you have will wear out. So you will go naked and I won't feel sorry for you." He went to the door and closed it. "Now," he said, looking at her, "you can take off that pitiful dress and get in bed."

He moved to a corner of the room, undressed quickly in anticipation and laid his clothes on a chair. When he turned to her, she was still clothed. "Do as I say," he ordered.

She began to cry.

"Lucia," he said, "I believe you are forgetting something very important. Apaches no longer attack the little settlement on the Mimbres where your family lives. Why is this? Because I arranged that through Ramos. In turn, we oblige them with guns and ammunition, horses and mules. But it's a tricky business. Apaches are hard to deal with. They always want more. I don't trust them far, they don't trust us far. Have you forgotten that because of me, *El Comandante,* your family is safe? Tell me!"

She was facing away, looking down. He took her arm and spun her around. "I've also tried to give you money for your family. Have you also forgotten that?"

"No, *señor.*"

"Why have you refused to take the money?"

"Because they wouldn't take it. Because they know . . . why I am here. . . . Not as housekeeper and cook as was promised. . . . Because I am only whore for you, *El Comandante.*" She was weeping again. "I am so ashamed. No boy will ever marry me. Everybody will know what I have been. Everybody in the valley. My life is ruined."

He tried to kiss her.

She turned her face away.

Angered, he seized her dress and yanked it over her head. She did not resist, just stood before him submissively, trembling, dreading. He nearly tore off her few underclothes. He filled his eyes with her —coal-black hair, deep brown eyes, fine-boned face. Her body as perfect as if sculpted in bronze.

He wrapped his arms around her, pulling her to him, but felt no response, no answer to his embrace or to his rising urge for her.

"Do something!" he said. "Respond, woman! Respond!"

She would not. Her tear-streaked face could have been cast in marble, so set and enduring it was, so devoid of any emotion.

He continued to indulge himself, hoping she would respond.

"Woman, come on! Act like a woman! Tell me this is good!"

She did not speak, nor did she respond the slightest with her body.

Finally, he gave up. She began dressing in quick, humble silence.

"You are very foolish, Lucia," he said. "I could give you many things. Someday soon I will leave here. When I do, I will take you with me. We'll go to Mexico City. You will have fine clothes and jewels. People will notice you. Men will bow to you—you are beautiful, you know. We'll see the world. You will like that, I promise you."

"Let me go. Please, *señor.*"

"No. Never."

She was dressed now. Without another word, she left him, her only sound the padding of her sandaled feet.

He didn't try to call her back, knowing it would be futile. He felt at loss as a man because she had not responded. No other woman had ever failed to do that before. But he would not have her killed like Roxie. No Ramos this time. He was reluctant to admit it, but he loved this simple but beautiful Mexican girl. Throughout his lustful and ruthless roving, she was the only one he'd ever loved. Lucia had spurned him from the beginning; she despised him—that was evident. In her simple, unresponsive way, she had won after all.

He spent the rest of the afternoon drinking and going outside the log house, watching the wooded pass where the wagons and riders would appear, hoping they would return early. But nothing changed. He was too anxious, he told himself, and too restless over his failure to resolve the matter of Colonel Taylor.

It was a little past dawn when shouts and the clatter of horses in the camp below the house shook him out of a wine-heavy sleep. Stepping to the doorway, he saw Ramos and the common Anglo horse thief and cow thief and killer of two Texas sheriffs who went by the ludicrous name of Abilene. They rode worn-out horses.

Only two riders out of six? And where were the wagons and drivers and guards? Something had gone wrong. Very wrong. The realization was like a physical blow. Never before had Ramos failed.

He watched Ramos and Abilene dismount at a tent where breakfast fires flamed and several men stood around.

His anger ripped loose. The worst had happened. He shouted for the cook. In minutes, he was served coffee charged with brandy. He drank a cup, then another.

He was in control of himself, in buckskins and cavalry boots, waiting in the main room when Ramos and Abilene came to the headquarters house. *At all times one in command must show dominance of the situation and of his men.* Fogel remembered that from his days as a uhlan.

Ramos seemed to hesitate at the open doorway, as he damn well should, Fogel thought, returning emptyhanded.

"Come in," Fogel said.

Ramos entered first. Abilene, a burly, quarrelsome man who reveled in wrestling bouts with lesser men and drank cheap whiskey out of a canteen as if it were water, stood aside, muscular arms hanging.

"I saw you ride in," Fogel said. "Only two riders. No wagons. It has the smell of disaster." But he would not blame his second-in-command now. Nothing would be gained. Gather all the information first. Ramos was too vital to the entire operation and the ultimate objective of Taylor. Besides, he had a murderous temper.

"Bad, *Comandante*. Bad. We lost the wagons—everything. Four riders, the wagon guards, the teamsters."

"That means all the goods we'd collected from the ambushes."

"Everything."

"Describe in detail what happened." Still in a state of disbelief, Fogel was having trouble reining in his shock.

"White Eye cavalry caught up with us and attacked, *Comandante*. I sent the wagons ahead and formed the riders. The White Eye fire was strong, *Comandante*. Never have I faced carbine fire that came so fast." He paused. He was a proud man and unaccustomed to defeat. "Four of our riders went down. Fast it was, *Comandante*."

"So you ran?"

"*Sí, Comandante*. It was that or die. That carbine fire—"

"It was concentrated fire, sir," Abilene spoke up, blustering. "Reminded me when I fought for the South."

Just long enough to desert after the first skirmish, Fogel had heard. Abilene was not the soldier he liked to boast about having been; however, he was utterly without conscience and important to the operation.

"You say White Eye cavalry surprised and attacked you," Fogel said, and smiled in a superior manner. "Of course, there is no other kind in New Mexico. The question is whether the cavalry came from Cummings or Fort Bayard, or less likely, from posts along the Río Grande, sent out on special scouting duty. It is strange. Not likely that they would have just chanced upon you. It was more like they were in hard pursuit and knew what they were after. . . . About what was the strength of the command that attacked you?"

Abilene avoided Fogel's eyes. "Eight or ten men."

"Eight or ten! Hell, that's only a small detail. Yet they made you run."

"It was the concentrated carbine fire, sir."

"Are you sure they didn't have a Gatling gun?" Fogel said, his voice dripping ridicule.

The Texan glared at him. "I told you they concentrated their fire. It was mighty rapid."

"Did you think of falling back to the wagons and maybe corraling them and making a stand?"

Abilene looked at Ramos, who shrugged. "No time, *Co-mandante*. They were upon us."

"Who fired first?" Fogel continued, beginning to doubt that anything would be gained through more questions.

"We did," Abilene said. "We couldn't let 'em see what was in the wagons, could we?"

"True. Yet it is strange that they seemed to be in pursuit of you." Frowning, he paced stiff-legged to the window and back, the heels of his boots striking the pine floor like mallets. Suddenly he faced them. "Where is Gat Shell? Why wasn't he with you?"

"Comandante," Ramos said, "do you not remember? You sent him to Mesilla to scout for the next wagon train." *You do not re-member because you were too taken with Lucia, who will never be yours*

willingly. Even lowly Mexicans have their pride. You are still a White Eye, Comandante.

"Clinch didn't go with him as usual?"

"No, *señor,* he was guard on one of our wagons. He was killed or captured. You yourself gave the order for him to go."

A shout from the camp broke Fogel's train of thought. Now what the hell? He stepped to the doorway. A rider was approaching on another worn-out horse. It was Clinch. He told Abilene, "Clinch is coming in. Get his ass up here on the double. Since he was with the wagons, he will know what happened there."

A dead-beat Clinch, urged on by Abilene, came weaving and puffing up the slope to the house. "Just gettin' ready to have myself a big ol' shot o' whiskey," he said all around.

"You can get drunk later," Fogel said. "What happened at the wagons? I want a full report."

"Ain't much to tell, sir," Clinch said hoarsely, grinning owlishly. "Them blue-bellies shot Mason an' Birch, ridin' guard in the other wagons, an' that white teamster, the new feller from South Texas that shotgunned all them passengers in the stage holdup. What's his name?"

"Brazos," Abilene supplied.

Glancing hopefully at a bottle of sherry on a table against the wall, Clinch said, "I surrendered. Hell, I had to. Them blue-bellies charged up fast an' surrounded me an' the Mex teamster. I emptied my rifle at 'em . . . knocked one blue-belly out of his saddle, but seen they was no way out after that." He stopped for wind, still hoping for a drink of sherry, but Fogel didn't oblige.

"Get on with it," Fogel said irritably. "So you surrendered. What happened to the wagons?"

"A young blue-bellied lieutenant an' a white man me an' Gat seen in Mesilla before we tied in with the Benedict train . . . reckon he was a scout . . . pawed through them wagons like a houn' dog diggin' out a rabbit. They seemed purty excited about what they found, you betcha." He looked directly at the bottle, but Fogel said, "Go on."

"They tied my hands an' we headed north with the wagons. When they questioned me that evenin', the blue-bellied lieutenant he threatened me big about contraband. Said I'd go on trial in

Mesilla." He was talking so fast he had to stop for breath. "That scout-lookin' feller he remembered me bein' with Gat an' bein' with the Benedict train, an' wondered why we wasn't killed with the rest of 'em. I said my horse went lame an' I dropped out, Gat went on. Said I made it in to the store near the fort, but I didn't mention Jacob Vane's name—no, siree. Said I didn't know 'im." He stopped again, hopefully.

Fogel said, "Recount your escape. Make it brief."

Clinch seldom had an audience like this, and here was his chance to look good in the eyes of *El Comandante*. "I took my time. Played possum on 'em till late that night. The blue-bellies forgot to search me. I had a knife in my left boot. I slipped it out an' cut myself loose, an' catfooted it fer a horse tied to a wagon. Whenever somebody stirred, I'd freeze. I tell you, sir, it took all my old-time savvy to slip outa that camp." He was going to extend the long-winded spiel even more, figuring the drawn-out account would improve his chances for a drink. "They was sentries ever'where. Just as I eased up to a horse—"

Fogel's abrupt motion cut him off. "I need only one more piece of information from you. This cavalry detail: what regiment and post?"

"Third Cavalry, Fort Cummings, sir."

Fogel slapped his thigh. "I knew it all along! Somehow that simpleton Taylor stumbled onto information. The detail knew what it was after. It was in hot pursuit."

"Maybe Vane spilled the beans?" Abilene said.

"He's too careful for that. He lost money, too."

"Maybe one of his whores?"

"What would a whore know?"

"Men talk."

Fogel rubbed the D-shaped scars on his bearded cheeks. He could feel blood rushing to his face. His pent-up anger, long simmering, seemed to burst out of him in a flood. His voice shaking, he said, "Taylor—and his stupid Irish micks. To think that they would intercept the biggest shipment we've ever had. They must pay for this—they will pay!" He whipped around. "Ramos, I want the post under strict surveillance. Not as we have been doing, most of the day. But all the daylight hours. From dawn till dark. *Comprende?*"

"*Sí, Comandante.* It will be done."

"I want two lookouts posted up close, so one can be sent back at once as a messenger. I want relay riders posted at intervals between the lookouts and headquarters. I want to know every movement of any kind that comes out of that post. If it's only the water detail, or a mail rider heading east, I want to know everything. *Comprende?*"

"*Sí, Comandante.*"

"Above all, I want that lucky simpleton Taylor dead. He must pay for this, and that's not all. I will find a way."

The time had come. A blaze of hatred twisted Fogel's face. An irrepressible fury demanded that he act. He would, and soon.

Thirteen

A uniformed Jaime marched into headquarters, answered the grinning orderly's salute with an equally snappy one and rushed into Colonel Taylor's office. His father, poring over reports, looked up and said, "Good afternoon, Sergeant."

"Papa," said Jaime, cutting short the formality and climbing into his father's lap, "I want to go riding, but Sergeant O'Grady says Corporal Daly's on sick report."

"Probably put there because you've worn him out." Taylor hugged the boy and kissed him on the cheek. "Tomorrow I'll have somebody else escort you. Run along now. I'm busy."

"No, Papa, I want to go now."

The Colonel gave him a stern look. "You'll have to wait. I promise you can go tomorrow."

"No!"

Taylor stood the boy up and applied a sharp tap to his buttocks. "No more of that, young man. Run along or I'll have the orderly escort you to your quarters for conduct unbecoming a noncommissioned officer."

But he didn't smile when he said it, and Jaime knew that he had lost his plea. Although the general gave in more times than not, he did have his limits, and once stated, he did not change them. Pouting, Jaime stalked out and went past the orderly without returning his salute.

Feeling put down and unfairly restricted, Jaime wandered to the stables to be with his closest friend, Patches, halter-tied in a stall. He brushed and curried the spotted pony. Then, on sudden impulse, he bridled him and laid on blanket and saddle, and after several tugs, cinched up. He was pleased with his work, a chore usually done by the escort trooper.

He led the pony out and stopped by a corral to watch troopers breaking a new horse. Four men had bridled, blindfolded and saddled a gray bronc, tied to a snubbing post. A young recruit-looking trooper climbed to the saddle. The handlers gave him the reins, snatched away the blindfold, released the snubbing rope, and horse and rider shot skyward. The bronc bogged his head between his forelegs and started bucking. Two jumps, and horse and rider separated, the recruit making a cloud of dust as he landed on chest and chin.

"Want to try 'im again, Flynn?" a handler yelled.

Flynn staggered to his feet, shook his head, wiped the dust off his face. "Ye domned right! I'll give 'im the devil's cure!"

Jaime laughed and wandered on, thinking of Corporal Daly. He liked and respected Daly a good deal. Daly was a good soldier. Was he really sick or was he just pretending so he wouldn't have to ride with him? Jaime feared the latter, which hurt his pride as a friend and fellow cavalryman.

An urge close to rebellion drew him to the post gate. The guard smiled and said, "Good afternoon, Sergeant Taylor," and threw a most correct salute.

Delighted, his depression lifting, Jaime said "Good day" and returned a salute in kind.

"Waitin' for yer escort, are ye, lad?"

Jaime scarcely knew what to say. He didn't want to lie, having been instructed sternly by his parents not to, and spanked more than once for "telling a story." So now, although saying nothing to the trooper, which actually cleared him of telling a lie, he just sort of moved his head in a way that could be taken either yes or no, and stood in the entrance of the sally port.

In the corral the handlers had snubbed the gray again, but the bronc was fighting and pulling back. A trooper grabbed the bridle on each side and held the wall-eyed head fast.

"Come on, Flynn. Get aboard!"

Flynn did, in a rush.

The freed bronc, learning from the first time, immediately lowered his head and appeared to break apart. And, as before, Flynn took off like a soaring rocket after two jumps and plowed up the dust on his face.

The handlers ran after the dangling snubbing-post rope, but the bronc eluded them and ran around the corral. The upper rail on the gate was down. Seeing more daylight, perhaps, the bronc banged into the gate and the other rails clattered down and the bronc broke out, running for open spaces.

The trooper at the post gate ran forward, waving his arms and shouting to turn the bronc back.

At that instant, as if obeying some hidden impetus he was unable to control, Jaime led Patches through the open gate and turned to his right. There, hidden by the high adobe wall, and still in the grip of the strange and impelling force, he mounted and took the trail to Cooke's Spring, feeling a heady sensation of freedom and exploration.

At the edge of the spring, he halted to admire the cool bounty. An errant breeze carried its fresh scent. The never-ending lifeblood of the post, the general said. A blessing for men and all animals. Jaime dismounted and, on hands and knees, holding the loose reins, he and the pony drank side by side.

Getting up, he wiped his mouth with the back of his left hand and gazed about. Mighty Cooke's Peak, which the general said was the noblest landmark in southern New Mexico, held his eye. A picture formed in his mind: *A horn in the sky*. To his left, northwest, he saw a much lower peak and wondered if it had a name. If so, he'd not heard it. It was shaped, he decided, like a Roman helmet he'd seen in a book. The thought fascinated him. From this day on it would be called Roman Peak. A little thrill ran through him. Today he had named a peak! That was the first thing he'd tell his father and mother and Corporal Daly. He must tell the corporal, who wouldn't take him this far.

He mounted, but did not rein away, listening to the muted sounds of the post, shouts, horses moving. Before long it would be time for the call to Stables. Red-wing blackbirds chattered in the brush on the other side of the spring.

He turned his eyes to the ruts of the trail winding toward the canyon, and hesitated. Maybe he should go back to the post now. He thought about that. But he wouldn't get this chance again by himself. He wouldn't go far. Just a little way, he promised himself. *Just a little way.*

He thumped the pony's fat flanks and trotted away, drawn again by his compelling impulse. It was more than mere curiosity. It was his boy's eagerness to search and see for himself so much that was new without the tight rein of an adult holding him back, forever it seemed. He passed the spring. The trail rose to wind through the foothills. The eager pony didn't seem to mind the slope. They rode like that for some minutes.

Jaime reined up, feeling his breath quicken. He could see a long way from here, the post and the tiny figures of troopers and horses moving inside the walls and the flag, the trace of the old stage trail snaking off for Mesilla like penciled lines. Cooke's Peak loomed before him, higher and closer, making him feel smaller and smaller. A red-tailed hawk sailed by. He was awed, struck with wonder.

He rode on, skirting the very edge of his promise, he realized. But everything was so vast and awesome. Up here he felt that he could see the whole world stretching away. Far off there was Mexico.

The post was getting much smaller, and he felt his first stab of loneliness. A cold fear brushed him. That was a funny-looking rock ahead. He would go on just a little way and look at it . . . *just a little way,* then go back. He rode on. The sides of the canyon weren't steep, but the trail was rough and there was a lot of brush.

He stopped to look at the rock. His mouth flew open. Why, there were carvings on the rock! Sticklike figures he thought resembling a deer and a man. Funny figures. Indians had made these! More to tell when he got back to the post.

But it was time to go. He reined Patches around and heeled him into a trot, and stopped.

Two riders blocked his way. Their faces scared him, mean, dirty.

One man grinned at him, but it wasn't a friendly grin. His teeth looked all broken and yellow.

A lump rose to Jaime's throat. He swallowed, said, "I'm going back to the post," and nudged Patches forward.

"You're comin' with us, gringo kid."

"I am not!" Terribly frightened, Jaime tried to fight back the tears, but they trickled just the same.

"Tie him on your horse," the other man said. "That pony would hold us up."

Jaime fought them, but they laughed at his puny blows while they tied him. As they rode off toward the mountains, he glanced back and the last thing he saw was the fading scene of the walled post and the flag flying above the guard tower, growing ever smaller. His eyes blurred. In his short life, he'd experienced only the little fears of a boy engrossed with himself, soon dispelled by a word or hug or kiss. Now a dreadful terror seized him. Would he ever see his father and mother again, and Patches, and Corporal Daly, and the other troopers? He feared not.

Jesse was standing in front of the sutler's store, around him the pleasant hum of the busy post. Retreat would sound in half an hour. He was still no nearer to a decision about leaving, alternately restless and becalmed, held here by the feeling of something left unfinished.

A shout shook him out of his musing. It was the guard at the gate, and he was holding a riderless Patches, Jaime Taylor's spotted pony.

"Sergeant of the guard!" the man shouted. "Sergeant of the guard!"

The sergeant appeared on the run.

"Where's Jaime?" the sergeant asked, eyeing the pony.

The guard threw up his hands. "The pony just now came to the gate. He's lathered. He's run some."

The sergeant crossed himself and became dead-still. A second later he ran for headquarters.

By now a milling crowd of troopers was gathering. Knowing what was coming, Jesse went to a corral and saddled the red horse. He was leading his mount out when Lieutenant Ayers reached him.

"What is it?"

"Jaime's pony came in without him."

"God—but there was no escort assigned to him. Corporal Daly's on sick call."

"The boy must've slipped out."

Ayers groaned, called out for Sergeant O'Grady, and hurriedly set about forming a search detail. In the confusion, troopers ran to quarters for weapons and then to the stables. Over all this Jesse caught the bellow of O'Grady's voice. A concerned Corporal Daly left the infirmary and stood by, looking guilty as hell for dodging escort duty.

Colonel Taylor rushed from headquarters. He quickly scanned Patches from head to tail. "How did Jaime get out without an escort?" he demanded of the sergeant of the guard, who turned to the crestfallen gate guard for explanation.

"Sir," he said, "Jaime led his pony out here and seemed to be waitin' for escort. About that time a bronc busted out of the breakin' corral. I ran up to turn him back. When I came back to me post, Jaime was gone. I thought he'd left with the escort."

"When was that?"

"About two hours ago."

"What direction did Patches come from?"

"I don't know, sir. Of a sudden I turned around and there he was." He straightened himself, aware that he was going to catch it.

"The question is," Taylor said in a voice that was the calmest here and held no censure, "where shall we search? Perhaps Jaime fell off. Yet, if he did, I don't think Patches would run off. He's trained to stand when the reins are dropped. Let's ride down the trail."

An abashed Daly spoke up. "Sir, Jaime's always wanted to ride up the canyon a little way. I never would take him there. I'd say that's where he went, sir."

With Taylor in the lead, they tore out along the upper trail. At the spring, they found the pony's small prints in the soft soil of the water hole's rim. Heartened, they spread out on the trail climbing into the rugged foothills, the colonel carefully retracing the pony's tracks. Now and then he and the troopers would call out Jaime's name. The silence seemed to mock them. They rode on, slower now. Light was fading with their hopes.

Dusk was a purple veil when Taylor halted the detail, staring down at a clutter of tracks in the middle of the rough trail, flanked on each side by brush-covered slopes.

"Jaime stopped here . . . maybe to look at something," he said, visualizing his boy's movements. "Maybe at those petroglyphs over there. . . . He starts to turn back—he pulls up here. Now horse tracks come in from this side of the trail. How many horses would you men say?"

O'Grady was nearest. He studied the tracks. "Two horses, sir."

"Now," said Taylor, "the horse tracks veer off . . . back the way they came in. . . . Patches, like any good pony with his rider gone, heads for home. Now let's spread out and see where the horse tracks go."

Calling Jaime's name, he spurred off into the brush.

In the gloom the tracks grew dimmer and the up-and-down going slower. The troopers kept calling.

Darkness was falling when the detail lost the tracks on a rocky slope. By this time the men had quit calling. Reluctantly, Taylor called off the search and turned back, but Jesse knew they would be here at first light in the morning.

After a glum supper with the enlisted men, Jesse was outside smoking when Ayers joined him.

"What do you think, Jesse?"

"Apaches have been known to kidnap white kids. Not many, I guess, because there weren't many chances. They've taken plenty of Mexicans. That's one way to replenish the tribe. Mexicans make Apaches faster than white kids do. I reckon it's because a true Mexican—I don't mean the mixed-blood *Mestizos*—is a Mexican Indian. Yet we've seen no Apaches around, have we?"

"None. Amelia Taylor is in shock. The women are with her."

"Poor lady."

They said nothing more for a time.

"I'll be with you when the search detail goes out in the morning," Jesse said.

"Good. I was hoping you would. Yet I was afraid you might be getting restless to ride on."

"I still am, but . . ."

"In the morning, then."

In the barracks Jesse made ready for bed, reflecting on an old piece of advice he'd heard he knew not where: Sleep when you can sleep, eat when you can eat, because there'll be times, sooner than you might think, when you can't do either. To that he added: Always ride a good horse.

He slept on that.

Good tracking light greeted the searchers at the place on the trail where the two riders had taken Jaime. Again, they swung away to the northeast, and again they followed the tracks to the rocky slope where the tracks had vanished.

Colonel Taylor pulled rein, studying the terrain. At his command they spread out to begin working in the direction of the mountains.

For hours, they carefully went over the ground, and found only a scattering of fresh tracks here and there, disappearing in a clutter of old tracks. Nothing seemed to lead anywhere.

Noon had come when Taylor, face grim, turned back. He ordered that the rest of the post's afternoon schedule be kept.

Now, Jesse thought, *the waiting starts, and with Apaches it may never end.*

At about three o'clock the guard in the tower called down, "There's a rider with a white flag. He says he's got a written message for the colonel."

"An Apache?" the sergeant of the guard asked.

"No, a white man."

A trooper went out and took the message to headquarters. Jesse followed Ayers in. Taylor was looking at a piece of paper. Enraged, he held the paper out to them. "Read this. It's the damndest, most outrageous thing I've ever encountered."

With Ayers, Jesse read:

> Colonel Taylor: I have your son. He has not been harmed—yet. You may have him back for 100 Spencer rifles or carbines and $10,000 in American dollars or gold coins—repayment for my wagons and merchandise your detail took.
>
> I expect your reply by this rider. Do not try to follow him, or your son will be shot.
>
> El Comandante

You will remember me as Corporal Fogel, the man you
unjustly branded, lashed 50 times, and drummed out of the
fort. I now have my own command, which would prevent any
foolish notions you might have about rescuing your son. You
are under constant observation.

"Clears up not one but several matters," Taylor clipped, fury
sharp in his eyes as Ayers returned the paper. "All along, we've
blamed the Apaches for what's happened on the trail, including the
Benedict massacre, when it's nothing but a gang of heartless brutes
led by a madman. I cannot allow him to throw down the gauntlet at
the U.S. Cavalry, even if the life of my son is at stake. In my reply,
I'll tell Fogel his demands are too unreasonable to be met, and for
him to return Jaime at once." He sat down at his desk to write, his
jaw set like a rock. His hand shook as he looked for pen and paper.

"Sir," Jesse said, feeling his way, "why not string this Fogel along
. . . tell him you'll try to meet his demands . . . but it will take
some time. That'll give us a chance to locate his camp in the mountains and get Jaime out of there. Fogel has to have a camp if he has
what he calls a command, and where else would it be around here
but in the mountains?"

"Those are mighty big mountains, Mr. Wilder. You could hide an
army in there."

"Yes, sir, but Fogel is in there somewhere and he makes tracks
going out and in."

"But how do we locate the camp? There's no trail that we know
of. If there was one and we went charging in there in daylight,
Jaime would be at risk."

Ayers said, "But we do have a trail, sir. The tracks left by the
wagons that stopped at Jacob Vane's that night."

"But that brings up back to daylight tracking," Taylor reasoned.
"Fogel's lookouts would spot us, just as they obviously did Jaime."

Silence gripped them.

"There's a full moon now," Jesse said presently. "If a man can
read a newspaper in the clear air of this New Mexico moonlight,
which he can, why can't he read wagon tracks? Send your reply,
General, and Lieutenant Ayers and I will get on the tracks tonight
with a little detail."

Taylor took that in without change of expression.

"The wagons came out of the mountains that night," Jesse said. "I believe we can find the camp."

"I see no other alternative," Taylor concluded, and began writing.

Afterward, at the colonel's direction, they set about making plans and studying maps. Ayers, thinking of veterans, asked for O'Grady and Daly in a detail of six. They would take extra dry rations and extra canteens, grain in saddlebags and a hundred rounds for each carbine. Once the detail located the camp, Ayers would send back a man at night to the fort. Taylor would take the command out, guided by the trooper, and be in position to attack at daybreak.

Simple, Jesse thought wryly, *with the usual unexpected complications. There were always some. You could bet on it.*

"Remember that your horse can see better at night than you can," Taylor said. "Trust him. For the same reason you see horses running in a pasture at night—they can see where they're going."

They left the post when the moon was rising full and headed east in the cool desert stillness. As Jesse rode, a late realization crossed his mind, that a new cause, this time a little boy's life, was a partial and needed release from his own past.

The hog ranch was dead-quiet, not a sound, seemingly deserted except for the one low light in the saloon.

"The old crook's settled in for the night," Ayers said as they reined toward the mountains. "But he'll open up when the devil knocks on the door for a drink of rotgut."

Jesse had to chuckle a little. "The last time I heard about the devil at the door was from an arm-wavin' backwoods preacher in Tennessee when I was a boy. Every time he stomped his foot, he'd raise dust. He'd a-whupped the devil for sure that day."

There had been travel on the trail since the night the loot wagons had stopped, and the detail didn't pick up the incoming tracks until some rods north of the adobe. The broad wheel prints were discernible enough at first as the troopers moved at a steady walk, at times a slow trot across the flat country, then winding into the foothills. This took considerable time.

But they lost the tracks when the great bulk of the mountains loomed before them and the tilting terrain changed even rougher. Apparently, the teamsters had detoured around a rocky outcrop.

Ayers halted and ordered his men to fan out looking.

They spent a good while searching, the horses stumbling over the rough footing, the *clack* of shoes on loose rock sounding alarmingly loud, until they picked up wagon tracks in a sandy arroyo slanting out of the mountains. Jesse could hear the lieutenant's sigh of relief. Up the arroyo they rode double file, walking the horses.

Roaming clouds masked the moon. Ayers halted. *Where*, thought Jesse, *was all the easy tracking he'd so confidently promised the colonel?* So they waited awhile.

The clouds moved on and the moon bore down again, glossing the way, making the night like glittery day. Only minutes had passed during the halt, but it seemed like a long time. Farther on, they saw the serpentine shine of a loquacious little stream. They watered their mounts, drank with them and rested them.

The tracks wound on, ever rising, lost sometimes in the gravelly soil, which caused brief delays. They weren't yet among tall ponderosa pines, Jesse saw, but rather the shorter piñon pines and junipers and stubby oaks. The big pine country was much farther north, according to post maps, in the Black Range, haunts of the Warm Springs Apaches. By no calculation could he see their mission taking them that far. Fogel, operating out of the moutains, would have found much easier egress and return by sticking to the lower elevations. But where was the camp? By now they'd covered some miles.

Ayers said nothing, but seemed of the same mind. He halted again, a question in the order.

After a bit, as if groping, he walked the detail up a slant, the horses blowing a little. The crowding, low-growing timber flanked them, shutting off some of the light on the wagon tracks. Jesse asked himself how far they had come into the mountains. It was hard to judge roundabout distance at night. How much time had elapsed since they'd left the post? He figured it was well past midnight.

The tracks led them out of the timber and suddenly, it seemed, onto a fairly level stretch of meadow bathed in moonlight. At the same time Jesse caught the sweet smell of juniper smoke. The troopers halted in their tracks as if struck.

Raucous voices raised in song to tuneless banjo music reached them.

Jesse could make out hooded wagons parked in a line. Above and beyond them sat a row of tents on the far side of the meadow, their order reminiscent of a military encampment. Figures danced around the tongue of a leaping campfire.

A man shouted, "Go to sleep, you god-damned night owls!"

"Go to hell!"

The revelry continued.

"This has to be it," Ayers said, low, "but I'd like to know where they're holding Jaime before I send a man back."

Jesse glanced at the sky and back at the meadow. "You're right. Be daylight pretty quick. We need to hunt a hole . . . and that looks like somebody on the other side of the meadow pacin' this way. Maybe a sentry."

They ducked into the timber by the trail, dismounted and led their horses back. When Ayers halted about fifty yards on, he and O'Grady left their mounts and moved back, Jesse with them.

When the meadow came into view, they saw that the guard had stopped. He was looking their way. They froze. About a minute passed before he paced on.

"He heard somethin', sor, but he's not sure, and the woods are dark," O'Grady murmured. "Appears he's makin' the rounds of the whole camp. Just one sentry shows they feel mighty secure up here."

"Good thing he wasn't here when we came out of the timber on the trail," Ayers said. "He may be back when it's daylight."

They settled down to wait.

The revelry had run its course. Nothing stirred in the camp. The guard paced by again, close enough so they could hear him yawning. He seemed to glance once at the timber where the detail was and went on.

"He's still curious," Jesse said.

Time seemed to hang until the sky changed from gray to pink and golden sunlight spilled across the grassy meadow. A large log house took shape upslope from the tents and a small cabin between the house and the tents. Horses and mules milled in two corrals below the wagons.

"Every wagon represents the lost hopes of a poor immigrant family brutally murdered on a trail they thought would lead them to the Promised Land," Ayers muttered.

As he spoke, men left the tents to start breakfast fires.

"A little later," he said, "let's get a head count on the number of men Fogel has. I can see twelve tents. Figure two to a tent at least. Maybe more. For now, let's take our mounts farther back."

They found a shallow canyon well back from the meadow for the horses. O'Grady, studying the canyon's dry floor with the eye of an old campaigner, chose a low, sandy spot and started digging. Within minutes he had dug out a pool of water large enough for the horses.

"And you did it without a forked branch," Ayers exclaimed. "You must be a water witch, Sergeant."

"It's the rainy season, sor. Otherwise, wouldn't be a drop. If we get thirsty later, there's always prickly pear."

Ayers posted the detail atop the brush-studded canyon wall facing the meadow. Below, timber covered the intervening distance to the wagon trail and the near side of the meadow. There everything lay in full view. It was time for sleep. Ayers and Jesse took the first watch.

The morning seemed to loiter. The sun burned away the coolness. Jesse caught himself nodding. Men moved about in the camp. After going to the log house, a man saddled a red roan and took the trail out of the mountains.

"Fogel's messenger, carrying the answer to the Old Man's reply," Ayers guessed.

A figure in buckskins and black boots emerged from the log house and paraded down to the tents, swinging his legs, knees locked. A saber trailed on his left side. He spoke to a group of men and paraded back to the house.

"Fogel," Ayers said.

"In goose step," Jesse marveled. "Can you beat that? Saber, too."

"He's right in character. O'Grady recalls that Fogel was sky high on himself as a military man, no less than a genius. Everyone else was beneath him. You could say he was about as popular as a skunk in the barracks just as Taps blows."

They began taking count of the men in the encampment as some fed horses and others went back and forth to the house. Others cleaned weapons and worked on horse equipment. Jesse sensed an air of preparation.

"I figure about thirty-seven men, counting Fogel and the messenger," Ayers said. "May be a few more in the tents."

"Sounds about right."

While they talked on, a rider on a powerfully muscled black horse dashed up the wagon trail and rode straight to the house.

Jesse stared. "Recognize the horse?"

Ayers was still looking.

"Benedict's black Morgan stallion," Jesse said. "See that big horse once, you never forget him."

"It is! And it has to be Gat Shell in the saddle."

"The same."

"Fills out the picture, Jesse. Everything's come together."

Not long before noon they saw a Mexican girl carrying a plate from the big house enter the little cabin. She closed the door.

Ayers snapped up. "That's where they're holding Jaime, by God! The girl is taking in food. A man in camp is watching her. I'd like nothing better than smashing in there right now to get the boy."

"I feel the same. We could make it to the cabin, but could we make it back across the meadow with thirty-some men firing at us? Better wait. Something's astir in camp."

O'Grady arrived with the next relief and Ayers and Jesse went back a little way where the others rested. Sleep came instantly.

Jaime flinched when the Mexican girl entered the cabin. He'd been crying and he tried to hide his face, turning away, ashamed.

"Poor little gringo boy," she said, placing the plate on the table. "I bring you food. You eat. You feel very good again. But first, you wash face and hands." She dipped water from a bucket into a pan and put it on a stand. "Wash," she said.

Jaime balked, even though her voice was kind.

A rough towel hung by the bucket. She dipped a corner of the towel into the pan. Bending down, she gently wiped his face and brushed back his unruly brown hair. He accepted the attention, but stubbornly squinched up his face so much she laughed, which he didn't like.

"Now you wash hands."

He refused.

"No wash hands, no eat."

He was hungry, terribly hungry. Nothing to eat since they'd kidnapped him, only some water. A guard had taken him outside twice to relieve himself. The rest of the time he'd stood at the single window, watching and hoping to see his father and the troopers riding up to rescue him.

Seeing his refusal, she took both his grubby hands and placed them in the pan and washed them and dried them.

"Now eat," she said, standing by the table.

Hunger overcoming his unwillingness, he sat at the table. But still he did not eat, just sat there pouting and looking at the beans and a strange-looking piece of something, round like a pancake but certainly no pancake. He sniffed and pointed at it. "What is this?"

She smiled. "Tortilla. Good. You will like."

He wasn't sure how to go about eating it. Seeing that, she tore off a piece. Scooping up some beans, she passed it to him. He ate tentatively the first few bites, then with a hungry delight he finished the tortilla and all the beans without protest.

"Good, gringo boy. You like."

His chubby face swelled. "Don't call me gringo. I don't like that name."

"What is your name?"

"Jaime—Jaime Taylor. My father commands Fort Cummings. He's a great soldier. He was a general in the Civil War."

"I will call you Jaime. But I no hear of your Civil War."

"What is your name?"

"Lucia."

He was feeling much better. Hers was the first kind face he'd seen. All the men were dirty and ugly and smelled bad. She was good to him and hadn't cuffed him around like one of the men when Jaime had refused to enter the cabin. His arm still hurt, but he hadn't shown tears for the man to see, not until he was alone in the cabin. He was only eight, but going on nine, as he liked to point out.

She was pretty, too, and clean, yet kind of sad, and she was smiling at him. He looked at her, hoping, smiling back at her, and he asked, "Will you be my friend, Lucia?"

It was his compelling smile that broke her. Suddenly she bent and took him in her arms and hugged him hard and held his face to hers. His fears, her fears. *My people love children,* she thought, *they have so many.* Her mind often strayed to her five little brothers and three sisters on the Rio Mimbres. At seventeen she was the oldest child.

Tears rose to her eyes, and when she looked at him, she saw his like huge raindrops.

"I want to go home, Lucia," he said, holding on to her. "Back to the post. Can you take me home?"

"I can't . . . but you will go home. Soon, I hope." She hugged him again. He smiled.

What a sweet smile he had, this poor little gringo, who would be killed with his father if *El Comandante*'s plan worked out, and there was nothing to stop it.

A shout from the house shattered her thinking. She turned in dread and stopped at the door. "I will bring you something to eat again, *amigo* Jaime. Something better."

A puzzlement cut through his happiness. "*Amigo,* Lucia? What does *amigo* mean?"

"It means friend, Jaime. We are friends. Remember that." She hurried out.

He felt better then.

Fourteen

Around four o'clock, when Ayers and Jesse had the lookout again, they saw the messenger on the red roan return and ride to the house.

"All the Old Man can do is dicker for time till he hears from us," the lieutenant said. "I'll send O'Grady and Daly back as soon as it's dark, with word where we think Jaime is and the size of Fogel's outfit. Two troopers will make more certain one gets there."

Across the meadow, men moved in and out of the tents. *Waiting as we're waiting,* Jesse thought, *except they know what Fogel will do.*

The two watchers stayed quiet, each sealed in his own thoughts.

"Fogel knows damned well that the general can't get hold of a hundred Spencers," Ayers said after a while. "In the first place, the War Department would never permit such a swap. If it did, it'd take weeks for the rump-spring geniuses, as he calls 'em, to approve it. I doubt, too, whether the rifles could be bought from the Spencer people—time's another factor there. As for the ten thousand, the Old Man might put together a few thousand at the post, with the sutler's help, but no more. Fogel knew his demands couldn't be met."

"I look for Fogel to demand a parley, on a site of his own choosing, of course," Jesse reasoned. "Right out there on the meadow, where he has the advantage. Where else? Nothing near the post."

"What Fogel wants more than rifles or money is to get the Old Man where he can kill him, even torture him. I think, too—and this keeps gnawing at me—that he plans to kill Jaime . . . before his father's eyes, to make him suffer more."

"My feeling is the same. The boy is in great danger."

Ayers peered through the binoculars again. "I've been noticing the guard at the cabin. Same man all the time. He watched the Mexican girl like a hawk when she went in and when she came out. . . . Seldom takes his eyes off the door. A wild-looking *hombre*. Long, bushy hair and beard. . . . Shuffles back and forth with a rifle. Swings his arms. Moves like a man possessed. . . . Or more like an animal watching his prey."

The slanting afternoon sun dropped another notch, banking more heat in the crowded junipers and piñons and oaks below. Yet time seemed to stand still, the waiting growing more burdensome.

"The general has to come in here," Jesse said. "But if he comes alone with one of Fogel's messengers, he's as good as dead. He and the boy both. I can't see Fogel agreeing to a military escort."

"No. Fogel's got all the high cards. Why wouldn't he play 'em?"

"But if the general storms in here with the command in broad daylight tomorrow . . . in the style of Kelly's Ford and Brandy Station . . . that, too, might spell the end for Jaime. I even hate to bring it up, but that's the way it looks to me, Tom. The hard reality of it."

Their conversation fell off by mutual consent, as if they wearied of it.

Ayers, looking through the binoculars, said, "I see three men leaving the tents. They're going to the house. The wild man is with them. Another guard is taking his place. Proves for certain where Jaime is."

Fogel put down the wineglass and was standing at rigid attention to impress them when they entered the cabin. Ramos, Abilene, Gat Shell, and the Wolf. Sebe, the messenger, a thick-set man with deep-socketed, flinty eyes under heavy dark brows, stood in the rear of the room.

Fogel waved a sheet of paper at them. "That simpleton Colonel Taylor wants more time to meet our terms. Says he is trying to get the Spencers from Fort Bliss, and has raised a few thousand of the ransom money. He is asking for a parley to talk things over, as he puts it." Fogel loosed an enormous belly laugh. "A parley, he begs, near the post. Does he think I'm a fool? I'll give him a parley, all right—the stupid blue-belly colonel. He will come here and he will come alone because he has no other choice, and then we will kill him out there on the meadow, and take what money he has on him. I never expected him to get the Spencers. Neither did I expect this to be so easy. . . . Tomorrow morning Sebe will take back my answer. The parley will be here. Taylor has no other choice."

"What about the kid, Cap'n?" asked the Wolf. He never got the rank right, which irritated Fogel. A short, wiry man, he wore an enormous prickly gray beard that stuck out like porcupine quills. The skin of his cheeks, what little could be seen, was a sickly yellow, and his eyes, likewise yellow, seemed to throw off sparks. His voice was hollow, his mouth in the thicket of whiskers like a trap that snapped rapidly when he talked. A scar split the center of his forehead, perhaps the result of a near-miss from a knife or hatchet. He never changed clothes; he wore them out. Fogel could smell him. He was constantly in motion, either swaying from side to side, or shifting his booted feet, from which the grimy toes protruded. The Wolf was waiting for instructions, it seemed.

"I thought I told you what to do," Fogel said.

"But if we kill the man first, we're missin' somethin', Cap'n."

"What do you mean?"

"Before we take care of the man, do in the boy. Let the man see it."

"How?"

The Wolf drew a long knife from his belt. The yellow eyes sparked as he made a slashing motion across his throat. "Be a sight for the man, it would, Cap'n," he said, emitting a strange "hee-hee."

Fogel rubbed the D-shaped scars on his cheeks reminiscently and nodded. "We'll do it your way."

The Wolf grinned and shuffled out of the room, stirring a wave of stifling stink.

Fogel looked at the others. "Any other ideas?"

Shell said, "I've got one," and ran a forefinger up and down his long, flat nose.

"I hope it's better than the news you brought back from Mesilla."

"Sir, word's got back plumb into Texas about the Benedict train and others, too. They's two trains markin' time right now in Mesilla. But they ain't budgin' without military escort."

"There'll be others," Fogel said. Nothing daunted him today, the way his plans were going. He'd figured all along that Taylor would have to come here for a parley. He had no choice because of the boy. "Well, what is it, Gat?" Shell was a phlegmatic and surly man, but once set on a certain course, there was no turning him aside. Hence, his value.

"I say before we kill the colonel, let's give him fifty lashes like he gave you. Let the boy see that, too."

Surprised, Fogel felt like bowing to him. For once, the dull Gat Shell had come up with an original idea. "Good. We'll include that."

Shell, who seldom smiled, cracked a poor imitation of one, he was so pleased with himself.

Fogel turned to Ramos. "Are we agreed, *señor,* on the orders to be carried out when the stupid blue-belly colonel arrives?"

"Sí, Comandante. As before, the parley will be near the wagons in the meadow. There will be riflemen in the wagons, hidden behind the hoods, if there is any trouble, and Taylor has men following him. The lashes will bring one change. But instead of looking for a Mexican *mulatero,* I will lay on the leather myself. It will be done as you wish, *Comandante."*

Fogel looked at Abilene, the sheriff killer, who shrugged and said, "Nothin' I'd like better than seein' the hide ripped off some blue-belly officer. Reckon I've fought enough of 'em."

Fogel felt the impulse to make an appropriately derisive reply, but withheld it. It was wise to feed the vanity of one's underofficers sometimes. He dismissed them with a wave and opened a bottle of sherry. In a few days, his objective reached, he would ride away for Mexico, leaving the band to its several factions. Without his strong hand, there would be a bloody fight for leadership. Ramos would prevail because he was utterly ruthless. Abilene would back him.

* * *

Lucia, in the kitchen, had heard each heartless voice. She slipped
out the back way to the woods, eyes to the ground, sick at heart.
She had known they were going to do it, but not this way—more
cruel than the first, while the boy's father watched. What could she
do? She had no weapon but her faith. She prayed then, as the village
padre had taught her to pray, on her knees, hands clasped, face to
the heavens, beseeching, tears tracing her cheeks. And somehow she
seemed to find an unexpected strength she didn't know she possessed. It seemed to come from beyond her. Maybe out of God the
Father's blue sky or carried on the wind, cool and clean, sighing out
of the mountains like a doomed child's whimpering to go home.

Much calmer now, she walked back to the house and looked into
the large room. *El Comandante* was opening another bottle of
wine. He would be drunk before long and would not shout for her
again, because he'd already violated her once this day.

She went about her duties, her mind closing on the dreaded tomorrow and the little gringo boy.

Dusk wasn't far away when Jesse, watching the meadow while Ayers
rested beside him, said, "I see possible trouble, Tom. They've set
out night pickets and one is curious, keeps looking this way. Probably the same one last night that might've heard something, but
wasn't sure. Now he wants to find out before dark."

The sentry stopped at the meadow's edge, looking all around. He
appeared to be debating with himself. Another moment, and another, and he seemed to shrug off any indecision and suddenly
walked into the timber.

Ayers said quickly, "We'd better get down there. We can't let him
come this far."

"You're in command—stay here."

Before Ayers could say more, O'Grady was there. "He's comin'
this way, sor."

Without a word, he and Jesse slipped down the slope into the
timber. On the way, they held up when they saw the sentry slowly
scouting toward them, his attention shifting curiously left and right.
They flattened out, waiting.

He was a stocky white man, his pockmarked face like chipped

rock as he came into closer focus. There was nothing here to arouse his suspicion. The horses were tied on the other side of the wall in the canyon. But, Jesse wondered, was that the *clink* of an iron shoe on rock? It was. But had the sentry, farther away, heard it?

If he had, he did not quicken his step. Still, he kept prowling, rifle ready, his slow caution showing suspicion of the ridge where the detail lay and what might be beyond. He left the forest litter and started up the gradual incline of the slope, causing a little clatter of loose gravel. He gave a start at the noise, halted and came on in the dusky light.

Jesse and O'Grady lay to the sentry's right, hidden under the low-hanging branches of a piñon. He was now slowly moving away from them, but still upslope. Unless they rushed at once, he'd have time to turn and fire, alarming the camp.

They looked at each other—NOW!—rose and charged, covering the distance in four pounding steps. Jesse, who was nearest, went for the man's rifle, hoping it was on safety. At the same time, O'Grady tackled the man around the hips and clamped a hand over his mouth, shutting off a yell. The three went down in a tangle, rolling down the gravelly slope. Jesse had the rifle.

The man had surprising strength. He wrenched free with a muffled snarl and came up with a knife from his belt while O'Grady fought to choke off his voice with one hand. Even so, he got off a smothered cry. Jesse crashed the rifle barrel across the man's skull. He grunted, dazed, but slashed back with the knife, missing as Jesse lurched clear. O'Grady, hacking for wind, grabbed and twisted the knife free and buried it in the man's chest with a solid *thunk* again and again.

It was finished as suddenly as it had begun.

They stood over him, looking down, winded.

Gravel crunched as Ayers reached them. "Can't leave him here. Let's drag him over into the canyon and cover 'im with rocks."

They did that.

Twilight thickened. The detail chewed hardtack and sipped from canteens. Cooking fires flared along the line of tents. No sign of alarm there. Instead, the contrary. A little early banjo music and a voice or two in ribald song.

"They'll miss him when they change pickets," Ayers said, "but where will they start looking? There's timber all around the meadow."

"Unless," Jesse said, "somebody saw him go in here. But I can't see them searching in the dark."

"They'll start for certain in the morning."

"They will, if there's any kind of military order to the camp, and there appears to be under Fogel. Leaves us two choices: get out of here or dash to the cabin for Jaime. And we can't leave the boy."

Ayers chewed a lip. "The Old Man has to bring the command up tonight," Ayers said flatly. "Not tomorrow night—but tonight. We're very close to running out of time. Our usefulness will be gone by morning. Too, it'll be close to morning before the command gets here, even with O'Grady and Daly leaving as soon as it's dark. How do you see it, Jesse?"

"The same, with one change."

"Speak up. I want to know."

"If the command's not here by daylight, we ride hell-bent for the cabin for the boy, win or lose. He's our main mission." Did he sound a trifle patronizing? He didn't mean to.

"Need you remind me, General Wilder, sir?" Ayers's tired voice was curt, close to outright anger.

Jesse drew back, stung. "You know god-damned well I don't have to, Lieutenant Ayers, sir."

An uncomfortable silence sawed between them, broken when Jesse got up and walked down to the canyon to see about the red horse, regretting what had just happened. Friction in the field. An old problem. Tempers on edge. Time an unrelenting pressure. Little sleep. Short rations. Men's lives riding on a single decision. The officer in charge playing God because it was his duty. He'd never served with a finer young officer than Tom Ayers. Well trained. Good judgment. Cool under fire. Companionable. Cared about his men. Sure as hell did.

He fed the red horse from the saddlebags, rubbed him between the ears and on the neck, and pulled up some grass to leave him. Climbing back to the detail in the last of the fading light, he found Ayers writing busily, his field book on one knee. He finished and handed the report to Jesse. "I'll appreciate your reading this."

It was addressed to Colonel Taylor and read:

Somewhere in the Mimbres Mountains
Sir: I have the honor to report the following:

  We have located Fogel's camp and the cabin where Jaime is
being held under guard, across the meadow from the detail
under cover in timber. We have counted 37 armed men in the
tent camp. We can see a park of immigrant wagons, and two
corrals of horses and mules. Fogel is here, dressed in buckskins.
His headquarters is the one large log house.

  Of immediate concern is a picket who approached our
location this evening. It was necessary to kill the man to avoid
detection. When they search for him in the morning, we have
two choices: to run or use all our efforts to rescue Jaime. Be
assured we will do the latter. In my opinion, the command
should be brought up tonight, at the latest by daybreak, and
attack the camp. At that junction, the detail will rush the cabin
for Jaime.

  To make certain this report reaches you in due time, I am
sending it by Sergeant O'Grady and Corporal Daly, who will
guide the command here.

  Respectfully,
  2nd Lt. Tom Ayers

"That's as clear as a man can make it," Jesse said, returning the
report.

Ayers called the two couriers and explained the contents of the
report. "Remember, the command has to be here by daybreak at
the latest. How long do you figure it'll take to bring them up,
Sergeant?"

"Four or five hours, sor."

At dark Ayers and Jesse accompanied the two to the woods by the
wagon trail. Seeing no pickets, they led their horses down a way,
mounted and rode off at a slow walk.

"There is something I'd like to say," Jesse began as they made
their way back through the timber. "It's that Lieutenant Tom Ayers
is in command of this detail, and that one Jesse Alden Wilder will
carry out his orders as far as humanly possible." He'd spoken quite
earnestly.

Ayers slapped him on the shoulder. "Why, hell, Jesse, I know that. No need to say so."

"I regret this evening."

"No more than I do. It's behind us."

In silence, they walked to the canyon's rim where they could watch the fires of the camp. The banjo player was at it again, without any chorus. Jaime's cabin prison was dark. A light burned in the big headquarters house where Fogel held forth.

Sebe, whose real name was Rube Yocum, avoided the usual roistering that night and went to his tent, thinking of the long ride tomorrow to Fort Cummings; besides, the camp was still short of women. Always had been, except for the few castoffs Fogel had brought in from Jacob Vane's. Fogel was lucky, him gettin' the young Mexican girl. When he tired of her, which didn't look soon, Ramos would get her. Or Abilene or Shell. Sebe had never had much luck with women. They always seemed to shy away from him, even the worn-out ones. Once one told him it was his scary eyes. Truth was, that pleased him.

Sleep evaded him. He'd grown uneasy of late. It was always the same: after some months in one place, it was time to look for new country. The specter of his past was always a few jumps behind him. Someday it would catch up with him, the family he'd murdered from ambush during the feud in eastern Kentucky. If he'd just killed grown men, it might not have mattered so much. But he'd done a complete wipeout: young girls and boys. Not all at one time. But now and then. Killin' was in the Yocum blood, his pap used to say. It was. He kinda enjoyed it and was proud of his marksmanship.

But he'd overlooked one important factor. The Tesh family had some distant cousins in South Carolina, and they had vowed to avenge the killings of their kin. Mountain honor. They'd purt near got him in the Missouri Ozarks. Might have if they hadn't been so likkered up. There was a little pack of 'em. He'd shot two, dead center, then got to his fast red roan, which he always kept saddled nearby. Someday they'd catch him with his guard down. It was fate. In Texas he'd picked up the name of Sebe. Most men here went by just one name, none of 'em given names. One name was enough. The Texas killers amused him, usin' names like Abilene and Brazos.

Another feller was Pecos. Another was Laredo. Some used the name "Tex." Tex who? And there was the real crazy one that called himself the Wolf, the one that guarded the little gringo kid. Even the Texas killers walked around the Wolf.

Hours later, after a restless night, it was dark when he saddled the red roan and crossed the meadow to the wagon trail. An early start would place him out of the mountains by daybreak with Fogel's answer to Colonel Taylor.

Around four o'clock, it must have been, the detail led the horses out of the canyon and into the woods facing the meadow. Jesse filled his pockets with shells from a saddlebag, in the event he couldn't draw a tube from the Quickloader, and watched the camp. All fires were out. Not a sound from over there.

Ayers looked at the sky and said, "The Old Man's gonna have to hurry if he makes it before daylight. How long do you figure?"

"About an hour," Jesse said.

Time lagged like a dragging weight.

The chock-chock of a horse coming across the meadow froze them still. Every man held a hand over his mount's nose.

The rider passed on down the trail at a trot.

"If that's the messenger, he's early," Ayers said.

"I wish we could get a better look at what's coming up the wagon trail," Jesse said.

They walked out to the trail and saw that a bulge of timber cut off an extended view from their position. Therefore, keeping to the trees, Ayers had them move the horses farther up trail and to their right. From here they could see directly down the trail. It stood empty in the moonlight, mocking them. Where was the general?

Sebe rode relaxed, an enormous wad of tobacco bulging one jaw, musing while the red roan eased along at a ground-eating running walk. His saddler had once belonged to a wealthy Kentucky horseman and tobacco farmer near Lexington. A stubborn man, unarmed at the time, he had resisted giving up his fine horse on the lonely country pike when Sebe stepped out of the shadows, and Sebe had to shoot him twice. The last time dead center in the forehead to make sure. The dead man's fat wallet had supplied food and forage for some time.

Riding alone in the moonlight, he was struck again by his uneasy feeling. Better call it a warning. He never ignored it very long. Sometimes he felt like an animal, his senses were so keen. All the Yocums was like that, pap used to say. Why they'd kilt so many enemies that needed killin' and lived to tell it. Like a man was supposed to live. Kill your enemies, else they'd kill you. Well, after he'd escorted the blue-belly colonel back here to his death, Rube Yocum would slip out and make tracks for faraway places. Utah or Idaho sounded right good. That's what he'd do. It was a wise man that follered his animal senses. Maybe, in time, he could even use his real name. He didn't like Sebe, but it was no worse than Abilene and Brazos, Pecos and Laredo. Or Tex. Tex who? He spat thoughtfully, amused again.

A sound pierced his rambling thoughts. He pulled up at once, peering ahead. A dark wedge filled the trail. It was coming straight at him. He bent his head, listening. Horses trotting. So many they made a rumble. Cavalry.

He whirled the saddler and spurred into a run.

Fifteen

Time seemed to rush by, now that daylight was close upon the detail. They watched the empty, moon-washed trail. Across the meadow, they could hear voices in the camp. Already breakfast fires burned.

"I guess," Ayers said, "something happened. Maybe Fogel's lookouts ambushed O'Grady and Daly. Yet I think both men are too experienced to walk into anything."

"There's still some time," Jesse said.

"Next question, when will the camp start looking for the sentry?"

"Pretty soon, Lieutenant. As soon as they can see well. If they're alert, they will. If there's any kind of order."

"We'll be at a disadvantage when daylight comes. Why not go for the cabin when there's still some darkness? What do you think?"

"The same. Whenever you give the word. But there's still a little time left for the command to come up."

Across the stillness broke the sound of hooves. Not those of many horses, however. Jesse saw only one rider galloping hard this way up the wagon trail. He bit off his disappointment, watching as the horseman cut across the meadow for the headquarters house.

"That has to be the messenger," Ayers said. "Something has turned him back of a sudden. He hasn't been gone long."

"Now he's shouting at the camp. Listen! Hell, he's giving the alarm. Means only one thing—the command is coming! He's sighted it!"

"Has to be. We'll still hold up a bit," Ayers said cautiously.

Fogel roused out of a wine-induced heavy sleep. Was that some fool drunk pounding on the door? Discipline had been too lax lately. He'd have to remind Ramos to enforce more order in camp by knife or gun.

"Who is it?" he called.

"Sebe, sir. They's blue-belly cavalry comin' on the trail!"

Sebe, one of his better men. Mean as hell, a born killer, but he would follow orders. Shock traveled through Fogel. He rolled out of bed onto his feet and slid back the wooden bar on the door.

Sebe rushed in, breathing fast.

"How big a force?" Fogel asked, already shrugging into his buckskins. He hoped Sebe realized that *El Comandante* was speaking in a calm and decisive manner.

"A big bunch, sir. They filled the trail, comin' at a steady trot. Wasn't just no little piddlin' bunch."

Fogel pulled on his boots and stood up, stomping his feet. "How far away are they?"

"By now about three miles or so, I figger."

"Go get Ramos. Hurry!"

Sebe dashed outside, but Ramos was already at the door and coming in.

Fogel met him with, "Sebe reports there's a large force of blue-belly cavalry heading our way on the trail. Approximately three miles away. Follow the ambush plan I've gone over with you. Post half the men in and around the wagons, facing the trail across the meadow. Post the other half across the meadow under Abilene, then join me at the wagons."

"*Sí, Comandante.*"

"We'll let them come in about halfway across the meadow, as planned. They'll be caught in between. An enfilading fire sweeping them from both flanks. The men at the wagons will open fire first.

Tell Abilene not to fire until he hears the roar of our guns. *Comprende?"*

"*Sí, Comandante.*"

Ramos bounded away, shouting orders as he ran to the camp.

Fogel buckled on his saber and put on his hat, thinking how he had prepared for this some time ago, in case Taylor should happen to slip past the lookouts. Although Taylor had done that by a night march, a surprise awaited him. A man with leadership qualities trained in military tactics foresaw all possible threats. So thinking, he walked out the door and past the cabin where the Wolf guarded the gringo kid. His men were already forming around the wagons, while others lined up for Abilene. Arms folded, he observed the orderly movements with approval. Daylight would arrive shortly. Anticipation was a sweet taste in his mouth.

Seeing the dim shape of the approaching lone rider wheel and race away, too fast and already too far to run down and capture, Colonel Taylor halted the command, his mind attuned to old battlefield reflexes and options, if any. He longed to smash headlong into the camp and rip it apart, but the element of surprise which he had planned on and hoped for was gone. To rush in now would endanger Jaime even more. The mere thought of his boy tore at him, demanding fast retribution. On one fact he could depend, the detail under Lieutenant Ayers, with the veteran ex-Confederate Wilder, would charge to the cabin at daybreak. Therefore, in timely conjunction . . .

Captain Frank Holt rode on his left, second in command. "Captain," Taylor said, "I think it's time for a little diversionary action at about daybreak. These people will expect us to continue up the road. They will be waiting for us in ambush, if this crazy Fogel has any sense of strategy at all. I want you to take Troop A and advance carefully up the trail, scouts ahead. Corporal Daly will accompany you as guide. There will be timber flanking the trail on the right as it enters the meadow. I expect their initial fire will come from there. Just engage, keeping up a steady fire, which should hold them in that position. If you encounter no resistance, swing to your left across the meadow. I will take Troop B and move off the trail around to your left. But, first, I need more confirming information from Sergeant O'Grady."

When O'Grady, in the lead with Daly, reined back, Taylor said, "Sergeant, the map you drew of the camp has the wagons in a line to our left in the meadow . . . the encampment of tents above and a little beyond the wagons. Next is the little cabin where Jaime is being held, then the large log house, which, apparently, is Fogel's headquarters."

"Yes, sor. That's the way the camp is laid out."

"Captain Holt, with Corporal Daly as guide, is taking Troop A up the trail to create a diversion at first light, expecting to run into trouble at or near the meadow. Meanwhile, I want you to guide Troop B through the woods below the wagons. At daybreak we'll pitch into whatever we find around the wagons and the tents. That should also put us in a line with the cabin, to drive on to it. At the same time, Lieutenant Ayers with his detail will be charging across the meadow for the cabin. Think you can get us through the woods by daylight?"

"Yes, sor, but we may have to dismount part of the way. The timber is thick. I suggest, sor, that to save time we continue up the trail some distance to a bend a few hundred yards from the meadow. Turn off there."

"Very well. From the looks of the sky we'd best get along."

Bustling sounds pulsed across the meadow to the detail, waiting on the edge of the woods. Voice raised in command. Tramping feet. Little by little a low blur of movement materialized. But no horses. . . . A bobbing line of men appeared hurrying toward the woods by the trail which the detail had vacated earlier. . . . The men disappeared into the woods. After that, a deep hush settled. A waiting.

"They've set up an ambush," Ayers murmured. "Fifteen or twenty in the bunch."

"Means Fogel has split up his men."

"The rest around the wagons, I'd say."

"I'd think so."

"Or the cabin."

"The worst turn," Jesse said, thinking of the inevitable snarls of battle. "But the cabin should not be Fogel's main concern. Having men on both sides of the meadow gives him a great field of fire. I've been wrong before. This Fogel's a crazy bastard."

"We need to warn the Old Man."

"How? We do anything now—jump the gun—and we tip off the camp before we can get to the cabin. I don't know, Tom."

"Just wishful thinking. The Old Man will know soon enough when we charge the cabin—unless he busts in here early. I haven't forgotten our main mission, General Wilder, sir." The last spoken in a light tone.

"Need you remind me, Lieutenant Ayers, sir?" Jesse replied in turn.

That eased the tension.

"I want us to be in the saddle before daylight," Ayers said. "On our way when light breaks."

"All right, Lieutenant. I'm halfway there now."

They watched the fast-changing sky. There was coming gray light trying to break through the roiling darkness, coming fast. The stillness around the meadow seemed to keep building.

"Prepare to mount," Ayers said, low but clear.

"Mount."

They swung to saddles and Ayers led off at a walk in a column of twos across the meadow, the drumming hoofbeats sounding unusually loud in the early stillness.

The sky began to turn a faint rose pink.

Ayers picked up the gait to a trot. Some distance before them, Jesse made out the dark bulk of the cabin. Beyond to his left, figures moved around the line of wagons. So he and Tom had figured right. Blood-crazed Fogel might be, vengeful Fogel might be, but he had posted his men well.

Gunfire erupted behind them, about where the trail entered the meadow. Jesse caught the bang, bang of cavalry carbines mixed with the sharper crack of rifles. Scattered red flashes split the darkness along the wagons. At that, Jesse saw a shape run from the cabin toward the wagons.

All at once, as if a massive hand had swept the sky clean, sunlight rushed hard across the meadow.

Ayers spurred to a gallop.

They pounded up to the cabin. Tossing reins to horseholders,

Ayers and Jesse ran to the cabin's door. Jesse kicked it open and barged in, eyes sweeping, Ayers on his heels.

The cabin was empty.

Both men stood stunned. They hesitated.

"The house!" Ayers said, and they ran out.

Something had gone wrong along the line of wagons. Scrambling down, Fogel's men faced about in milling confusion toward the lower woods. Out of that tangle surged blue cavalry charging hell-bent in column of fours, bringing the beginning bang of carbines. Jesse thought he glimpsed Colonel Taylor and Sergeant O'Grady in the lead as he and Ayers struck for the log house.

The door was shut. Both threw shoulders against it and charged in. . . . Empty. They plunged into the next room—the kitchen. . . . Empty. They ran to the room behind it—a bedroom. . . . Empty.

In dread concern, each saw the same fear in the other's eyes. Had Fogel murdered the boy?

A girl's scream broke their inertia. They rushed outside.

Jesse whooped when he saw a Mexican girl and Jaime standing on the rim of a wooded arroyo. She screamed again, pushing Jaime behind her with one hand while she held up the other in a helplessly protective way.

Toward them raced a wild scarecrow of a man, knife upraised.

Ayers and Jesse fired together. The wild man staggered, but kept going. They shot him again. The bullets drove him back and down. They ran to him. He reared up, still gripping the long knife, snarling like an animal, scratching and clawing to reach the girl and Jaime.

Jesse kicked him back, then shot him between the wild eyes and the snarling face blew apart.

The detail closed in around them like a shield, troopers and horses, Lucia still holding the boy, he clinging to her. Ayers ordered the detail to start firing, and the air turned acrid with burned gunpowder.

The intense milling and fighting around the wagons broke off as some troopers rode down their foes. Fogel's men started dropping weapons and surrendering.

"Hold your fire!" Ayers ordered.

Jesse saw Fogel, distinguished by buckskins and black boots, break out of the smoky confusion and run for the corrals. A trooper took after him. When Fogel slashed out with the saber, the trooper shot him twice with a revolver. Fogel dropped to one knee. Sinking down, he shouted in a parade-ground voice heard above the tumult, "I am *El Comandante!* Hear me, you blue-bellies! I am *El Comandante!*" He waved the saber once and collapsed.

A man on a speedy red roan raced away from the corrals. Two nearby troopers gave hot pursuit. Closing in, they shot him out of the saddle. The roan ran on.

Firing ceased as troopers herded prisoners together. Across the meadow gunfire dwindled, then died.

Colonel Taylor rode up to the detail and dismounted, the light of battle still blazing in his eyes. Jaime ran to him, sobbing and shrieking, "Papa—Papa!" Taylor threw his arms around him and held him fast. Then, in more great excitement, Jaime led his father to the Mexican girl. "Papa, Lucia is my friend. She wouldn't let the bad man get me."

Taylor held out a hand to her. "I thank you with all my heart, *señorita*. You are very brave. What happened here?" he asked, looking around.

"When shooting start and the Wolf leave cabin to see, I took Jaime and we ran to the arroyo."

"The Wolf?"

She pointed with horror, halting, weeping a little. "He saw where we go. He was going to kill Jaime. *Comandante* told him to. We could run no more. Then your soldiers come and shoot him . . . this very bad man, who kill many people."

"Where is your home, Lucia?" he asked in the kindest of voices.

"On the Mimbres."

"We will take you there when we get back to Fort Cummings. Bless your brave heart."

After Captain Holt's troop brought in more prisoners, order prevailed. Jesse and Ayers walked over the strewn field around the wagons where the hottest fighting had occurred.

"Another burying detail," Ayers groaned. "Only this time the enemy will do the digging."

Passing the huddled prisoners, Jesse caught a familiar owlish face. It was Clinch, as unconcerned as if nothing had happened. He was talking to a grim-faced young trooper in his wheedling, fawning way, showing that loathsome gapped, yellow-toothed grin. As a chameleon changes colors, Jesse thought, Clinch could be everything to all people. Whatever it took to survive. He would, somehow.

They came to Fogel's body, which looked overdressed, even theatrical, now in the fancy buckskins and black cavalry boots.

Ayers observed, "The Bard of Avon wrote that the evil that men do lives after them. In this case, I think we can say that the evil that Fogel wrought died with him."

"We know now," Jesse said, "what poor Junius Russell saw that horrified him so, left him speechless. Brute white men—not Apaches—murdering whole families. Women and children. . . . I've wondered, too, what happened to the younger women before they were murdered. And the voice Russell kept hearing—that had to be Fogel's, the craziest killer of all."

Between the wagons and the corrals, they found Gat Shell's body.

"He was making a run for Benedict's black Morgan and didn't get there," Jesse conjectured. "We know that Shell and Clinch spotted wagon trains making up in Mesilla and sent word ahead to Fogel. They must have signaled somehow to set up the ambush for the Benedict train after it left Slocum's."

"Evil attracts evil," Ayers said.

"All this has made you a philosopher, Tom."

"I'll say this. I've told you that I stopped feeling like a brash young second lieutenant fresh out of West Point long ago. At this moment I feel like a file closer of forty years."

"You'll get over it in time. A man has to go on."

As they turned back, Jesse said, "Ramos? What about him? Myth or real? Now's the time to find out once and for all." He went up to a surly prisoner. "Is Ramos in your outfit? Or is there a Ramos? If so, point him out."

The man sneered and deliberately, with pleasure, it seemed, jogged his head in the direction of a body sprawled by a wagon. "Ramos," he said, and spat on the ground. "Ramos."

"What part did Ramos play in all this?"

The man sneered again. "He was Fogel's lieutenant, and more. If a man tried to quit and slip off to the settlements, tired of all the killin', Ramos tracked him down." He spat again. "Ramos."

They crossed over there, looking down at the sharp-featured face, frozen in hate, the black hair down to the shoulders, at the red bandanna headband and the buckskin shirt, breechcloth and moccasins.

"I've never seen so much venom in a face," Ayers said.

Taylor ordered everything burned—cabin, log house, tents—the corrals torn down. "I don't want a single vestige of this evil place left standing to blemish the beauty of these mountains," he told his officers. Told that the bag of gold coins found in the house belonged to families in the Benedict train, he said the Army would hold it to be sent back to authorities in Arkansas.

By eleven o'clock the command was in motion. With Lucia and Jaime in the lead wagon, the wounded and the prisoners in others, troopers drove the loose horses and mules like a remuda. As they started down the trail, the red roan nickered from the woods and trotted out to join his friends.

They pulled into the post as the last notes of Retreat sounded. Jesse made himself scarce after feeding his stock. A cavalryman's bath, supper with the enlisted men, some drinks at the sutler's, and bed. For once, everything had gone well, which could be attributed to training and battlefield experience and determination. The general, instead of rushing headlong up the trail into Fogel's ambush, as Jesse and Ayers had feared, and which would have been characteristic of the dashing brigadier, and possibly disastrous—had slipped around through the woods and hit Fogel's flank. Great luck, also, when brave Lucia grabbed Jaime and ran to the arroyo. Otherwise. . . . For a reason beyond him, as if he must ever be reminded, the past played across his mind like a series of lightning flashes. Had it all been for nothing? The war, the prison camp, wearing the then-hated blue in the West, training the Juáristas and joining their cause? Losing Ana and their unborn child, and friend Cullen? No, it wasn't for nothing. There had to be a purpose. Father Alberto, that great little man, would tell him that was so.

On those thoughts, he drifted off into deep sleep.

*   *   *

Morning.

He had fed the red horse and packed the patient mule. Now it was time to say good-bye, his feelings mixed.

"You don't have to go," Ayers said. "You know that. You can stay as civilian scout." A crooked smile. "Believe you know the country well enough by now."

"I know. I appreciate it. I'm obliged to you all."

"Then why go?"

"I can't really answer that, Tom. Restless. Maybe driven. Maybe searching."

"I hope you find it. Good luck."

They shook hands.

"Good luck to you and sweet Eleanor. You'll make brigadier for sure."

"Maybe first lieutenant after twenty years."

Colonel Taylor came over to shake hands. "Well, there's nothing as hardheaded as an ex–Johnny Reb. We've tried every inducement to keep you here, but to no avail. We need you as scout and we need you to help transport the prisoners to El Paso. The Texas Rangers and U.S. marshals will find much to interest them in this collection of brute killers. They should all hang. Jacob Vane is also going along in irons. I look for him to be charged as an accessory. Some of these men say they will testify against him." Taylor's battlewise eyes took on an extra keenness. "Meantime, I'll be working on my history of Mexico's war with the French. In that connection, General Wilder, could you possibly shed light as to the source of those mysterious Spencers that the Juáristas used so tellingly?"

He waited, confident, Jesse saw, that the truth would come out at last.

"Well, sir, as I told you, our weapons came from many sources along the border. But I can tell you that the Spencers were very effective—very effective, indeed." He turned to mount, and as he did, the red horse danced a little, in that independent way he had. With a wave, Jesse Alden Wilder rode out the post gate and took the trail west.

ABOUT THE AUTHOR

Fred Grove has written extensively in the field of Western fiction, from the Civil War period to modern quarter-horse racing. He has received the Western Writers of America Spur Award five times—for his novels *Comanche Captives* (which also won the Oklahoma Writing Award and the Levi Strauss Golden Saddleman Award), *The Great Horse Race,* and *Match Race,* and for his short stories "Comanche Woman" and "When the Caballos Came." His novel, *The Buffalo Runners,* was awarded the Western Heritage Award by the National Cowboy Hall of Fame, as was the short story "Comanche Son." He also received a Distinguished Service Award from Western New Mexico University for his regional fiction, including the novels *Phantom Warrior* and *A Far Trumpet.* He is a contributor to anthologies, among them *Spurs West* and *They Opened the West.* His most recent Double D Western was *Bitter Trumpet.*

For a number of years Mr. Grove worked on various newspapers in Oklahoma and Texas as a sportswriter, straight newsman, and editor. Two of his earlier novels, *Warrior Road* and *Drums Without Warriors,* focused on the brutal Osage Indian murders during the 1920's, a national scandal that brought in the FBI. It was while interviewing Oklahoma pioneers that he became interested in Western fiction. He now resides in Silver City, New Mexico, with his wife, Lucile.